A WARRIOR'S HEART

AMANDA MCINTYRE

"A tender tale of the Old West"
~Hope Tarr, author of *LORD JACK*

To courage in the face of adversity, kindness in the face of hate, and the tenacity of heart—we are the survivors.

PROLOGUE

My Dearest Sarah,

This land is untamed and yet rich in its natural bounty. There is much to gain in being at the forefront of a new frontier. Brutal and savage as the terrain may be, its rugged beauty and resources will provide for us the kind of future deserving of a properly educated young woman. Thus far the natives have been peaceable, almost amiable in sharing the land and the gold found in the upper river basin. A group of us have formed an alliance to watch over each other in case there should be an unfortunate turn for the worse.

But I would prefer to speak of lighter things. I am most anxious for your arrival, as are the mothers of the few children in our settlement near what the Cherokee call the Sixes. I am certain you will find your new pupils eager to learn and most are well disciplined.

I've seen to it that your comfort is a top priority with Captain McKenna. He assures me that the route he is taking will be the safest and least difficult for this journey.

We will have little contact in the weeks ahead, but I place you in the capable hands of the Captain and his soldiers leading this new group of settlers to our new home.

Until then, God speed and stay well,

With love,

Papa

CHAPTER ONE

Late Summer 1837

Sarah clicked shut the delicate clasp of her burnished gold locket, a gift sent to her just six months after her father left last year for northern Georgia. It was a present celebrating the turn of her eighteenth birthday. This year she would be traveling during her birthday. Not that it mattered to her. What mattered more was being reunited with the only remaining family she possessed.

She lay the torn and wrinkled parchment note on the olive brocade bedspread and set her mind on what she had packed.

A breeze whispered through the open window of her boarding room, fluttering the curtains in almost a ceremonial farewell. Sarah stared at the twilight beyond hearing the soft thud of hooves followed by the carriages on the main street below. Tomorrow she would leave this all behind, not knowing when or worse, if, she would ever see the civilized world again.

Her father had bid her to stay behind to finish her training at Miss Emma's boarding school. It was one of the elite first schools in Waterford with the mission to "Improve female education." Her best friend, Emily, was Miss Emma's grandniece and on more than one occasion, their mischievous pranks were graciously overlooked by the blue twinkle in Miss Emma's eye.

She would miss Emily's companionship. Together they'd stayed awake at night, sneaking into one another's rooms to whisper about the future. Emily would likely remain in Waterford and no doubt marry a well-to-do young man befitting her name. Sarah, on the other hand, had a different view of what type of man she sought in a husband.

"He has to be strong," she lifted her chin in emphasis, "but gentle at the same time, and filled with courage and spirit."

Emily's brow arched as she bit off another piece of the ginger cake bread they'd stolen from the kitchen pantry. "You don't ask for much, do you?" She covered her mouth as the crumbs fell to the bed sheets.

"He'll love only me. I want to be cherished and respected…for my mind." Sarah tore a piece of cake and popped it in her mouth.

"And what of other things?" Emily purred with a devious grin. "What about your relationship—physically?"

Sarah's cheeks warmed at the thought. Not that she was immune to such musings. She and Emily had shared secrets of a similar kind many times over. Now with her departure imminent, the unknown and untamed world ahead appeared to hold more of the type of man more obsessed with finding gold than with cherishing a bride. A part of her feared she would die an aging old spinster, never having known the joys of marriage. "Of course, there is that. But Emily dearest, there are *other* things to be experienced in the throes of wedded bliss."

"And those would be?"

Her friend gave her an innocent look, capturing Sarah's solemn gaze for a moment.

Together they collapsed in a fit of laughter, only to be reprimanded by the stern voice of Miss Clara.

"Glory be, are you two at it again? I suppose I should be taken' you to see Miss Emma, but seein' how it's late and everyone is retired, I'll let it pass this one time." She tried to keep her expression stern in effort to intimidate the two girls perched on the bed, their legs tucked beneath them.

Try as they might to appear contrite to their wrong, they could not hold in a fit of giggles that spilled forth, much to Miss Clara's surprise.

"Off with you Emily Wilcox, get on back to your room and if I catch you in here again after hours, well, I'll—"

Emily sashayed brazenly past Miss Clara checking over her shoulder to give Sarah an evil grin. "Dream well, Sarah Jane."

"You'll be needin' these I'm thinkin' once the winter winds begin to blow."

The day had finally arrived. She was leaving New York. Sarah glanced over her shoulder and found Miss Clara turned holding up a pair of gray woolens. She folded them carefully and handed them to Sarah.

"These things are dreadfully rough, causing my skin to itch like fire. Sarah reluctantly accepted the clothing hoping she would have no need for them. She grimaced as the coarse material slid over her skin.

"Just the same, they'll keep you warm whilst in the wild, Miss Sarah." Clara glanced at Sarah with a frown and sighed, "What manner of father would be calling to fetch his daughter to an untamed territory with the onset of winter? Tis beyond me." She huffed as she rounded the bed, pulling down the coverlet and fluffing Sarah's pillows. "Taking his only daughter to a place filled with wild animals and worse, savages," she mumbled under her breath.

Sarah smiled softly as she poked and prodded through her bag, seeking a spot for the uncomfortable undergarment. "Papa says that most of the Cherokee are intelligent. Why, they have their own alphabet and some tribes, their own primitive government." She glanced at her companion, the closest thing to a mother she'd known over the past seven years. Sarah realized she would miss Clara most of all.

Attempting to ease her own fears, Sarah continued, "Papa says that, while he does not condone it on a personal level, there have been a few instances where a Cherokee woman has married a white settler."

The shocked look on Miss Clara's face at any other time would have been a delightful prank, but at the moment it did not serve to quell the deep-seated fears taunting Sarah. What would be worse? To die an aging spinster or be married to someone who wore barely any clothing? She chose to leave further speculation to simmer at the back of her mind, as she quickly stuffed the woolen pants in her carpetbag.

"Jesus, Joseph, and Mary," Clara muttered as she moved in front of Sarah. She grasped her hands tight. "Please tell me that you will be careful. What wee bit of boxing I taught you and Emily." She burst into tears and hugged Sarah tight to her ample bosom.

Unable to breath, Sarah lifted her face as the older woman's tears splattered on her cheek. "I will remember everything you've taught me, Miss Clara. And I promise to write, although you will need to be patient. I have no idea how often the mail will get through to you here."

She pulled free of the woman's stronghold and held her at arm's length. "Besides, if Papa believed I would be in danger, he would not have sent for me."

Miss Clara sighed, wiping the tears from her rosy cheeks. "'Tis a good thing he has put you in the company of Captain McKenna and his troops. At least he was thinking with a clear head when he did that."

Sarah cast her gaze to the ceiling, her attention drawn to the beveled glass prisms adorning the kerosene lamplight. Tomorrow morning, before the sun peeked over the tops of the few buildings along the main street, she would be well on her way to leaving all of this behind. And to what end? What kind of land lay beyond the pristine walls of Miss Emma's finishing school? What dangers lurked amid the deep forests, blazed only in recent months by a smattering of white settler's?

A shiver ran the length of her spine and she hugged herself to ward off the chill. She was not a weak woman. Nor was she prone to fainting spells or feeble knees. "It will be a new adventure, Miss Clara. I'm going to teach the children of the men and women of the *new* frontier." She managed a courageous smile, yet on the inside, a flurry of nerves assaulted her bravado. She'd been strong before in her life, surely she could be so again. Besides, she was older now and much better equipped emotionally for life's little surprises. "I should be getting my rest. We leave at dawn. Where am I to meet the Captain?"

"At the supply store, Miss Sarah. He'll be sending someone to fetch your bags early in the morning." Miss Clara turned, her skirt layered over a multitude of petticoats swooshed over the polished wood floor of Sarah's private room. She paused at the door, turning with a wistful smile. "'Tis a brave lass you've turned out to be, Miss Sarah," she said as she held her gaze, "If only your dear mother could have— "Clara turned her head, hiding a sniffle, and then turned back to Sarah. "You've got her courage, darlin' girl. It will serve you well in the days ahead. Peace be with you, child."

Miss Clara hurried over once again, wrapping her arms around Sarah in a fierce hug. Then she was gone.

Sarah dropped her bag near the foot of her cherry wood four-poster bed. She ran her hand the length of the cool, silky coverlet. Since the time of her mother's passing she'd been treated like royalty, especially by her father. Sarah often wondered if his attention was prompted by his materialistic tendencies, or simply his guilt.

She'd been told her mother had died of complications derived from the birth of her stillborn son. A son that Charles Reynolds had wanted, nay, longed for. Instead, he achieved only a daughter and two days after burying his son, his wife died leaving him with marginal hope of another son. Or at least a temporary setback, Sarah would come to find out most unexpectedly....

∞

One dismal rainy afternoon, Sarah had stumbled upon a small group of girls chatting in the parlor. So new was the death of her both her mother and brother that Sarah still wore her dark mourning dress.

"I heard she killed herself."

The brash comment caused Sarah's breathing to cease. She pressed her back into the shadows of the half-opened door and listened, with a sick heart.

"Why would she do such a thing?" Another girl replied, the tone of her voice indicating surprise. No more than Sarah at this moment.

"*They say* he had a lover." The young woman relaying the secret lowered her voice to a whisper, as though it was a delicious morsel to be savored.

Sarah's knees weakened at the very thought of her father producing such a hideous crime against her sweet mother. Her very being shuddered in weary sorrow and she wondered if the rumor were true and if so, would her mother have taken her own life to escape the shame? Regardless, the information was much too much for a twelve-year-old's still grieving heart. After all, the dirt on both her mother's and her baby brother's graves were still fresh.

A single tear slid silently down Sarah's cheek and she brushed it aside in anger-much as she did the unsolicited information she'd just received. The incident did not serve to bind her to her father, however and moreover created in her a greater independence that seemed well suited for her father's long business travels and her new home at Miss Emma's.

The gray-blue of twilight dimmed to a deeper shade of indigo as she prepared for her last night in the comfort of the room where she'd spent half her life. Pulling on the soft cotton gown over her head, she memorized its familiar scent of laundry soap used by the housekeepers. Brushing her palms over the front she realized that she was no longer a girl, but a young woman. Thoughts of her and Emily's past conversations teased her memory. Had she any hope of finding a husband in such a wild and forlorn place?

She crawled beneath the covers, pulling the layers of quilted blankets to her chin and settled her body to the warm comfort of the feather-ticking mattress. Many a night, its billowy softness replaced the comfort of her mother's warm breast. In the splay of the blue-white light of a midsummer's moon, she took one last look at her room, her safe haven and said a prayer that her mother and brother would watch over her on her new journey. Tomorrow, life would change—perhaps forever—but tonight she would commit to memory all she'd known as secure and stable in her world. Tonight however, she would not dream of her home, but of a hazy specter riding fearlessly on a great horse.

CHAPTER TWO

Misguided Trust

"Cut across the river and catch the villages on the other side." Their leader spoke in a low, commanding tone. "Do what you have to."

Their horses pawed at the ground nervous and edgy, like the rebellious men astride them and they whinnied and snorted impatiently.

"Don't use the torches until you get near the village, we don't want them to see us coming."

"Just a warning, right, Captain?" The gold tooth of the black-clothed rider glinted as he smiled. A random moon-beam peeked through the clouds illuminating the group of men.

"Don't call me that." Their leader muttered fiercely, "Be sure your faces are covered with your kerchief, and keep your brims low."

A voice uttered from the back of the group, his voice was not as confident as the rest. "Sir, is this to be the last raid for a while? There are those in the ranks getting suspicious of our intent." There was a hesitant pause, and then he quickly punctuated his sentence, "Sir."

"Those yahoos in Washington don't know what we face out here with these savages every day. Why, at any time, one of them could turn on us, on one of our children, or our women." He knew he had to bolster the men's confidence to instill in them that they were executing the proper justice for a noble cause. What indeed could be more noble that the progress of free white men? "Besides, these few remaining aren't cooperating like the others. These have to be shown and not told that the United States government means business."

There were quiet mutters of affirmation among the men, and there was no disputing whether what he said was true or not. After all the man knew the territory like the back of his hand.

"Any more questions before we split up?" He pulled the reins of his dark horse around and adjusted his kerchief above his nose. "Pull down whatever is hanging in the open." He paused, "There's to be no killing. Our cause can't afford it, but if you run into a situation where you have to defend yourself—" He left the sentence open on purpose.

The moon hid behind long smoky fingers of dark clouds as the men prepared for another midnight raid. They had a mission. That which the United States government had failed to accomplish with all its debates and legislation, this small band was implementing on their own. They looked upon it as their patriotic duty towards the progression of United States citizens.

"God speed, and watch each other's back." He dug his heels into the horse's side and sped off across the clearing with three men at his side.

"I don't feel right about this. I have a feeling we're stirring up a hornets' nest something fierce." The man who lacked confidence in his leader's decision spoke bluntly among those left in his wake.

"We don't get paid to think, Jeb. Just to do the job.

Now stop your bellyaching and let's get this over with."

"I nearly ran over a woman and her child last time." The same man's voice shook with fear and concern.

"You're welcome to stay here and wait for us, if you see fit to not take part."

The two remaining men were silent, waiting for the man to decide. To stay behind meant being vulnerable to an attack by those red varmints sneaking around the woods. No, he was smarter to go along. He'd just be more careful this time. After all, they weren't supposed to hurt anyone, just scare them so they'd give in and leave on their own.

"Let's ride." He pressed his horse forward, adjusting the brim of his hat as he flew toward the river.

There was much White Eagle knew of this land. His people, known as the Bear Clan, had made the hills of this territory theirs for more than seven generations. Like the blood coursing through his veins, he knew every river, stream, and creek that spread like a spider web across the terrain.

He dropped from his horses back landing with a thud on the moss-covered ground. Slapping the great Appaloosa's flank, the animal took off in a gallop as if knowing he should hide until called by his master's whistle.

Crouching amid the barberry bushes dotting the underbrush of the rough trail, White Eagle waited without making a sound. His gaze sharpened as he scanned the trail, and he knew he would not wait long to receive a sign from the great Creator.

His ears piqued at the faint sound of small twig snapping in the distance. Slowly, his movement swift as the wind, he stood turning to the sound. Raising his bow, he set his sight on his target and without hesitation let the arrow fly from his fingertips. The steady thrum of his pulse beat rapid against the corded muscle of his neck as he waited in reverent silence. The gentle thump that followed soon after indicated he'd made his mark. A slow, satisfied grin curled the corner of his mouth. He stepped from behind his cover, startled to find Tsula standing further down the trail, perched majestically on his ghost white horse.

"You've done well, White Eagle. Our people are fortunate to have such a great warrior as well as a provider." Tsula shifted on his steed, prodding the horse forward and followed as White Eagle climbed over a fallen tree to claim his kill. His gift of a keen eye and quick arrow was something White Eagle was grateful for. He'd decided long ago that it was a blessing to be used only for providing the necessary provisions for his people. The thirst for blood was not in his veins.

Dropping to his knee beside the fallen deer, he gave thanks to the Deer Spirit for a good hunt. He turned to see his Native brother, Tsula sitting proud and tall. He'd long admired and respected him for his intense loyalty to the tribe and his fearless attitude.

"It is with favor that I have pleased the Great Spirit this day." White Eagle stooped down, placing his palm firm around the base of the arrow protruding from the animal. He felt no pulse beneath his hand and with one swift pull, removed the arrow, wiping it upon the grass at his feet. Rising from his haunches, a ray of warm sunlight fell across his flesh and he breathed in deep, at peace with his past, his present, his——

A chill ran over his arms and he gazed into the face of Tsula. There was a time when he'd been able to be at peace with all three of life's phases, but now questioned his future and those of his people. And he wondered what role Tsula would have in that uncertainty.

Little by little, the white settlers trickled in from the coastal regions. Each sought their fortune in panning for the gold in the rivers near the Cherokee villages. Thus far, only a few scattered along the rivers, keeping peaceably among themselves, but White Eagle had heard the rumblings of discontent. The night raids of the faceless men tormenting the women and children in the villages by the light of the midnight moon had created the need for his people to watch the children more closely. No longer did they have the freedoms to play and hunt in the woods as when he was a young boy.

The settlers had brought more than conflict with them as well. They also brought disease to the tribes they settled near. In total, it was enough for Tsula to muster a small, but loyal following, whose meetings they kept secret from the peace council.

White Eagle brought his rough fingers to his lips and gave a shrill whistle, which was followed by the sound of thundering hooves.

The Appaloosa stopped short of the deer, a cloud of dust rising from the pawing of his hoof. He bowed head as though nibbling on a clump of grass, but it gave White Eagle pleasure to see the animal showing respect for the does sacrifice. At least, some codes of honor remained the same among certain creatures.

White Eagle lifted the doe in his arms, his muscles heating to the strain, compensating for the dead weight.

Laying the animal across the horse's back he tied the carcass effectively around its midsection. Grabbing a fistful of the Appaloosa's silvery white mane he pulled himself astride the horse.

"The white man has made our hunting more difficult. Their guns are faster than our arrows." Tsula pressed his heels to his horse's side, pulling the reigns to the side to fall into step with White Eagle.

His spirit quickened to the sound of settlers arguing among themselves, close to the bank of the river, their voices carrying upstream. White Eagle wondered how it was such a race survived if they showed no greater respect for one another than this. Though he'd not attended some of the council meetings, he sensed transition even at that moment.

Tapping his heels to the horse's side, he turned and grinned at his good friend in an attempt to dismiss the dread chilling his soul. "Still, they are not as sure with their guns, as we, with our arrow."

Tsula chuckled quietly.

In times of peace, Chief Silver Deer resided over the tribe. In times of war, Tsula would serve as chief of the war council. Each served in this way to allow clear-minded decisions for the good of all the tribal communities. Tsula had not been called upon to act in a time of war, and it didn't take the Shaman to tell White Eagle what was churning in the young warrior's spirit.

In the past week, the night raids had become more frequent and bold, destroying the campfires and tipping over the racks drying the meat being collected for the winter. Though the settlers were the suspected party, it was unclear which township or band of destroyers was responsible. Whatever the reason, it served to intimidate and instill yet more fear into the otherwise peaceful tribe. Each day more and more were added to the numbers emigrating further west, driven from their homes with promises of food, clothing, and new homes.

Chief Silver Deer, his tough skin weathered and tired, sat in silence at the head of the council ring, his spirit communing with the wisdom of the Great Creator. Finally, he looked up, his knowing gaze traveling from one tribal council member to another until it came to rest with White Eagle's gaze.

"Silver Deer, perhaps it is time to allow Tsula to take head of the council." A tribesman standing near the hut opening spoke openly, almost in challenge.

White Eagle's gaze darted to his friend's stoic expression. The heat radiating from the council fire muddied his ability to clearly see what Tsula's eyes revealed, but his intuition cautioned him that his friend was waiting for his chance to retaliate.

"We must concentrate now on gathering food and skins for the winter ahead. These matters cannot escape the wise eye of the great chief of the white people. Our people in Washington City will speak for us. There will be a resolution and it will be without war."

One of the peacekeeping council members threw his cup to the floor and stood. His eyes blazed with defiant anger. The Cherokee had always been given the freedom to speak their minds and his obvious disagreement with Chief Silver Deer was evident.

"This will not be resolved as your say, Chief Silver Deer. Already they move our people from their land. You have heard of the long huts where our people are kept in pens like cattle until it is their time to leave. We must protect our tribes and ourselves. You can smell the greed in the current of the mighty Chattahoochee."

Tsula's gaze skipped past the disgruntled warrior and settled with peaceful diligence upon White Eagle's as if to say, "*I am not alone in this.*"

"Perhaps Silver Deer is right. Chief Ross has requested a delayed removal of our people. We should not do anything that might endanger what he has achieved." Tsula kept his gaze locked to White Eagle's.

The irate warrior spoke with greater determination, his voice bouncing off the walls of the hut. "There is no stopping their greed. They will not stop their stripping of our land, our integrity, until they own every inch of our native lands."

Tension radiated from the clans leaders. White Eagle understood their anger, but it was laced with vengeance and that would likely get more of their people killed.

Tsula pulled another dreg of his smoking pipe, "Tomorrow we will form a hunting party and search for food." He pulled back from the fire, his eyes glittering in the heat. "I believe we will have much success in what it is we seek for the good of all. Whether we stay another season or whether they move us—"

Angry shouts rose from the circle of men.

"Let them try."

"This is our land, we will not move." Shouts of approval followed.

Tsula raised his hand and the room quieted. "We will need food and as always, our tribes have remained united. It is no different now and perhaps even more important. You must join us, White Eagle. Your keen eye and quick bow will be needed for our success."

White Eagle nodded, but a cold hand closed around his heart.

"You've heard from the governor again, I presume?" President Van Buren settled back in his favorite leather chair. Odd that it was so cold and damp already in late August. He stared at the flames in the fireplace. His present dilemma included the reports of certain bands of Cherokee, unwilling to leave and move to Arkansas, even when offered the means to start new lives elsewhere. For weeks, since John Ross and his delegation arrived in Washington, they were relentless in their pursuit of creating a new treaty for a small faction of Eastern land Cherokee.

"Yes, sir. Shall I read it to you, sir?" The militia messenger stood straight, bearing the folded parchment, his eyes focused forward.

Another dull throbbing began in his head. He had them more often these days and he made a mental note to see to the Presidential physician later.

"If you would." He waved him on and settled his hand over his brow massaging as he waited for the inevitable bad news. Not that his administration had been engaged in nothing but bad news since he took office a few short months ago. There were times when he missed Hannah. Times like now, she had a way of helping to see all angles of a matter.

"It is from the Georgia delegates, sir." The man cleared his throat. "Those Cherokee still residing in Northern Georgia are becoming rebellious, dare I say, nearly defiant in their attitude with the government. We are not sure what they may do next, but they strike fear in our citizens.

One of my appointed colleagues reports behavior that is both stubborn and cantankerous."

Van Buren sighed, ushering the man to continue.

"More reports are filtering in daily, most offer the same. Defiant behavior exhibited by the Cherokee. One of our men in Harnageville has requested we send federal troops to build forts for its white citizens." There he took a deep breath. "Respectfully yours, Governor Gilmer, State of Georgia."

Van Buren wished for the days when his life was simple. There was much to think about before he could meet with Ross and his delegation. Perhaps he'd been too hasty in thinking that Ross had control over his people. The idea that he could use him to make his people understand dwindled to a flicker even now.

Van Buren stood and leaned a hand to the mantle as he stared into the fire.

"Will that be all, sir?"

Forgetting he was not alone, Van Buren blinked and nodded, then cast his gaze to the deepening twilight through his window.

With the disastrous state of the present economy, if there was one problem he didn't need it was an uprising from a group of uncivilized Indians.

"Sergeant?" Van Buren turned toward the door.

"Sir?"

"Find me the Commissioner of Indian Affairs."

"Yes, sir." The soldier saluted.

Van Buren listened to the click of the door as he departed.

CHAPTER THREE

The Journey

"Your father gave me charge over your comfort, ma'am. His express orders were to see to it that you rode in the wagon." Captain John McKenna held the stern gaze of the irate woman glaring at him.

"And did my father also tell you I am an accomplished rider?" Sarah countered his staunch protocol with defiance. Her father had not been keen on her learning to ride; fortunately, Miss Emma had other ideas. "I'd prefer a horse to the stiff ride of a wooden seat, sir." Sarah stood, carefully folding the quilt, and placed it as a cushion for the solid pine seat. She heard the Captain clear his throat and turned abruptly, nearly losing her balance.

"I can see you have an exquisite—er—equilibrium, miss." The Captain tipped his hat, offered a rakish grin.

"I assure you my wit and my mind is quite sharp, sir, as well as my abilities on a horse."

"Indeed, I'm sure they are, but humor me will you? Poor Bixby has only the sight in one eye. I'd be obliged if you would see fit to ride alongside him, just to offer your expert assistance should it be needed."

The look in his eye skimmed this side of mockery, but Sarah could not argue that if she were needed in this way, it would be her duty to assist—this time. "Very well, Captain. You shall have it your way for now." She straightened her velvet jacket across her shoulders. It was a riding jacket sent to her from her father upon her announcement that she'd completed riding lessons. Though there'd been no note accompanying the gift, she took it as affirmation of his pleasure in her accomplishment.

"We should reach the first settlement by nightfall, ma'am. There you can freshen up and sleep comfortably on a real bed. Meantime, should you need anything on our journey, please send word with one of my men and I will try to accommodate you." He tipped his hat in a gallant gesture and turned his horse to ride ahead of the band of travelers.

Sarah sighed as she watched him ride away, and then glanced around her, drawing back the white muslin sheeting that kept the cargo from plain view. Inside she discovered a young woman, most likely in her teens.

"Hello, I'm Laura." The woman's smile was shy as she stretched out her hand to greet Sarah. On her lap slept a small child, scarcely a few months' old

Her puzzled expression must have shown all too clear as the woman offered a knowing smile.

"My husband is one of the soldiers. We're going only as far as the fort, and then we'll stay on. He's been ordered to duty there." The woman fingered the blanket, securing it around the baby's tiny feet.

Sarah's heart went out to the young girl, barely a woman. How brave she was to bring a child on such a perilous journey and how strong her love for the man she followed.

"How's Isabelle?" A low-timbered voice issued from the back of the wagon. Laura's husband, dressed in full uniform brought his horse near the end of the wagon and peered into the back.

Sarah noted each polished button on the front of his jacket, finding the contrast between father and soldier one that she would need to write in her journal. She wondered briefly how many other young families awaited her in the new settlement.

She dropped the curtain, letting it close to allow the family its privacy. A tinge of jealousy pricked her heart and it surprised her to think that she was envious in some small measure that this woman had already found such incredible happiness at such a young age.

Sarah tugged at her jacket, wondering if the day might prove to be too warm for it. Perhaps it was a simple case of the jitters or—she took a deep breath—perhaps she was anxious to get started on this new journey.

And while she'd never gone so far than girlish thoughts about the future and finding romance, she wondered if she would wind up like the young woman, married to someone in the military. Perhaps a high-ranking soldier...

"Are you comfortable, ma'am?" Captain McKenna stopped alongside the wagon touching a finger to his hat.

"As much as I can expect, I believe, Captain. Are we nearly ready to depart?" Hoping she would not give away the anxiousness eating at her patience.

He grinned, a charming expression brightening his handsome face. For a moment Sarah's heart quickened.

"Yes, ma'am. Whatever the lady wishes." He touched his gloved hand to his hat's brim, and then with a clicking sound, he prodded the horse to a majestic gallop toward the front of the procession.

The seat tipped to the side and Sarah reached out haphazardly, grasping for the iron rail to prevent her from lurching to the side. The feather of her new traveling hat slid to the side obscuring her view.

"Mornin' ma'am." An older gentleman with scraggly white chin whiskers climbed without finesse into the seat beside her. He grabbed the reigns and eyed her with a smile. "Goin' to be a right fine day for travel." The absence of three teeth greeted her in a friendly black gapped smile.

Sarah nodded, assessing the man that would be her constant travel companion for the next days. She tipped her hat attempting to adjust it correctly over her full coiffure Miss Clara insisted she wear for her special journey. "A proper young woman travelin' alone should not be presentin' her hair hither 'round her shoulders."

Emitting a frustrated sigh, she yanked off the hat all together, tucking the pin inside its felt brim. She'd nearly forgotten there was someone beside her.

"First time?" The aging man glanced sideways, coughing up a wad of black chew and thankfully spitting it the other way. He wiped his mouth on his flannel shirt.

Sarah held down the nausea rising in her throat and forced her view ahead. Captain McKenna rode with superior form and for a scant moment, she wondered about his ability to waltz in that uniform.

Another deep cleansing of his throat pulled Sarah's attention back to her travel companion. He gazed at her with one scrutinizing blue eye. The other was a silvery haze in color. Sarah wondered if it was diseased or some sort of injury that had caused his blindness. In either case, she hoped it wouldn't affect his ability to maneuver the wagon.

She concentrated on his good eye. "This is my first trip from New York, sir."

His laughter cackled in the morning air, followed by a coughing fit that brought up yet more chew. "Somehow I had a feeling it was, ma'am. Not to worry though, you've got one of the finest traveling companies assembled here. No problems with these boys around."

Something in his statement chilled her, giving way to curiosity. "Have there been problems for travelers?" She swallowed the tight knot of fear in her throat and remembered his chew. She was sick to her stomach all over again.

"No doubt these boys are prepared with many things to offer in trade with any *injun'* that is curious about our passage." He nodded towards Captain McKenna. "That man knows his way around these people. No cause for worry."

Sarah glanced worriedly at the small scar near the man's poor eye, suddenly not wishing to know from whence it came.

She clasped the small purse on the seat beside her and pulled from it a cloth covered journal. Emily had given it to her with a packet of writing tools as a going away gift.

"You must keep a diary of this adventure, Sarah. When you arrive at your destination, think of the stories you'll teach the children."

And the stories they will teach me, Sarah added mentally.

Emily had been almost more excited about this journey than Sarah. "There is one condition though, dear friend. You must send this back to me for I intend to publish it one day when I turn to my journalistic career. Promise me, you will do this for me."

Linking their pinkie fingers, as was their tradition for the most serious of promises, Sarah agreed to keep a detailed account and send it to her friend. She clutched Emily to her, breathing in the sunshine scent of her hair. Would she ever see her again?

Sarah stared at the book and clung to the handrail as the wagon jerked forward bringing her back to the present. Her journey had begun and she would do well to stay alert so at days' end, she could record her thoughts carefully. At least when she wrote, she and Emily would be close, if only in spirit.

As the wagon jostled over the lumpy mud road, Sarah took note of the men, women, and children just beginning their day. A cry from the back of the wagon startled Sarah and she pulled back the curtain to offer assistance to Laura.

The young mother smiled as the babe latched hungrily to her mother's breast. The unexpected picture mesmerized Sarah in a moment of curious fascination. When she realized her ill manners she glanced away embarrassed, averting her attention elsewhere.

"It's all right, Sarah. It's not a shameful thing, you know."

Sarah knew she spoke the truth and yet her inexperience in such things left her confused and curious all at once. Diverting her thoughts, she spoke candidly, "Aren't you afraid of what may be out there?" She nodded towards the child. "For her, I mean?"

The young mother touched the curly blonde ringlets surrounding Isabella's cherub face. "I know what it would be like if we were separated from her papa." She looked up catching Sarah's gaze with a serene smile. "We will travel this adventure together. You've no reason to fear the unknown." She reached for Sarah's hand and squeezed it confidently.

For the first time in many years, Sarah longed for her mother.

∞

The mist hovered low to the ground, an ethereal shroud blanketing the earth. To the trained eye it was a telltale sign of winter's eminent arrival.

White Eagle sharpened the flint of his arrowheads, concentrating on the task as the morning dew made the stone slippery and even more precarious to deal with. The fine scraping sound echoed loudly in the morning quiet. On most days, the sound and the stillness would give him great comfort.

"It will be a good day for hunting, my brother." Running Doe, his young sister appeared from the mist, kneeling beside him with her wooden bowl full of grain to be fashioned into the day's bread.

"Provided the Creator finds it worthy to shine down on us today." He kept his focus on his work. His dreams during a fitful night had left him restless, on edge. For many hours he lay awake on his pallet, tempted to visit the Shaman for an interpretation, deciding instead that to do so might create unrest for others, as it had for him.

"Your eyes are troubled." Running Doe halted her cooking preparations and narrowed her gaze to his.

White Eagle knew his sister possessed a keen intuition, especially when it pertained to her older brother. At times, it was a blessing; at other times like now, it cursed him.

He shrugged; perhaps he could dissuade her, "Have you seen Tsula this morning?" White Eagle did not have to look upon his sister's face to know her gaze was assessing. A moment of silence followed, broken by the sound of a flock of geese honking overhead.

"I saw him earlier. He was preparing for today's hunt." Her voice lowered to a whisper.

White Eagle's attention snapped to his sister's gaze. In that moment, they both knew that today would bring more to their people than a quest for food.

"Running Doe." White Eagle took a breath as he searched his mind for the right words. "If anything should happen today, I want you to take our people to the mountain caves. Leave this place and go to where we played as children. There you will be safe."

He paused, waiting for her reaction.

She nodded and to his surprise, did not argue.

He gathered his weaponry and tamped them to the ground into a neat bundle. After sliding them into his deerskin quiver, he hooked the strap over his shoulder.

"What about Tsula? You know I have chosen him. Had you forgotten that, my brother?"

He closed his eyes in an effort to gain perspective on the situation. Tsula was of the Wolf clan, cunning, quick, and less tolerant of the new settlers along the river panning for gold that once only the Cherokee knew of. White settlers now flocked to places along the river, wedging themselves in between the tribal villages and bringing with them disease and unrest.

Worse, Tsula and his followers had spoken often of taking revenge for the killing of Cherokee tribesmen by white men years earlier. In order to satisfy the ghosts of the dead that wandered the earth, unable to go yet to the next world, the balance put aright only when responsibility was taken and restitution given. In essence—restoring the balance of nature.

White Eagle knew his sister had much to learn about her intended, but because he was the next of her family alive, it was his responsibility to represent his sister in this matter. His job as *e du j* to her children would be to educate his nieces and nephews in the spiritual and religious beliefs of the tribe. It would also mean that Tsula would be bound to him as family.

White Eagle shook his head, "I cannot speak for Tsula. His future is his own."

"You will look after him; will you give me your word on that?"

He rubbed his rough palm over his cheek and sighed. He would sooner fight a grizzly. "I will do what I can, my sister. He is a strong man with a strong spirit."

Her smile in return was wry. "Then you should have no trouble understanding him." Running Doe's smile flattened to a thin line. "What troubles you this day?" She mixed small portions of water as she worked forming sticky dough in the bowl.

White Eagle stared at her hands, marveling at her craft. She did not take her eyes from his. It was as though her fingers were her sight, and she was able to measure both quantity and quality through them. He wondered if all women possessed such a gift.

"There is much division among our clans."

She shrugged, "And so it will always be, but we have found ways to heal the divisions. Marriage for example." She flashed him a pleasant grin.

He stared dumbly at his sister's flamboyant grin, wishing for all the gold in the Chattahoochee that marriage alone would quell the simmering thunder about to roll across this land. Still, he would not convey these thoughts to her and ruin her joyful countenance. "Perhaps you are wise in this, little sister. Perhaps Tsula is over-anxious about the thought of his betrothal." His tone teased her, kindling the exact response he'd hoped as he watched her cheeks blossom a pale crimson.

Dodging a slimy wad of dough, he laughed as he came upright, catching her steady gaze. It softened to a serious interest and he understood why she was aptly named.

"Be careful, my brother." Her warm brown gaze shone with concern.

Reaching down, he looped a muscled arm around her and gave her a quick hug, hoping to dispel the disturbed look in her eye, wishing he could only do the same for himself.

CHAPTER FOUR

Tempest Noon

Tsula's horse pawed at the ground hardened by the light frost over the past few nights. A thick red stripe was painted down the center of the great animal's head, another vertically drawn upon his chest. Both horse and rider's attention honed in abruptly as new riders joined them from various directions.

"Everything is ready." The scout pulled in his reins, his eyes flashing a similar darkness to the animal's fierce gaze.

"Good." Tsula responded, shifting the quiver of arrows positioned over his shoulder.

"What is ready? Have I slept too long this day? Have we already tracked our first kill?" White Eagle slowed as he approached the small group of tribesmen. Some of the men he recognized, while others he'd only seen in passing at council meetings. Something uneasy churned in his gut as he scanned their faces.

"It is only preparations for the hunt, my friend." Tsula waved off the riders, dismissing them to the woods.

White Eagle did not miss the signs of war paint on their horses as they fled into the darkness of the forest. He turned to find Tsula gazing at him, with a smooth white smile.

"What has kept you this fine morning? Look the mist already lifts with the rising sun."

White Eagle shifted; glancing at the warrior he once

called his friend. Where a reminder of his childhood memories once was, sat a man whose gaze White Eagle did not recognize.

"Where are the others going?" His gaze quickly scanned the ring of the forest clearing. He, Tsula, and the strange scout warrior were all that was left.

"In position for—"

Tsula cut off the warrior. "A great herd of deer," he interjected too quickly, waving a hand to dismiss his young follower.

"Your horse is dressed for battle." Cold dread seeped into White Eagle's chest. What was his old friend planning? Worse how was he going to stop him if his suspicions turned out correct?

"It is good for the tribes to know who the war chief is." He turned his horse, prodding him forward toward the narrow trail winding through the trees. It would take them near the river where white settlers had fashioned a crude road for traveling.

White Eagle hung back assessing his options. He knew Tsula was planning a raid on someone and there was little doubt that it was planned for the white man.

"Tsula," White Eagle hoped to reason with him.

With his face shielded by the shadows of the trees, Tsula spoke over his shoulder, "Do not speak your reason to me, White Eagle. Our people have been terrorized for many nights. Each day more men come. They strip our rivers and land in their greed. They give nothing back to the earth that they plunder." His voice rose in agitation, "They will not be satisfied until there are no Cherokee left. This man and his band of thieves must be stopped."

The truth was painful even to White Eagle, yet it was

not his people's way to initiate war. "It is not our way. The council has not agreed to war." He prodded his horse riding along side of Tsula, hoping to reason with him.

Tsula turned to him with a placid expression. "This is not war, my brother. We are merely giving them a taste of what their people have given us."

"It is not wise," White Eagle insisted. Rapid concern skittered up his spine. The admonition to his sister blazed with full clarity in his mind.

"Perhaps, but we can no longer ignore the fearful cries of our children in the night." Tsula gazed at him with a gaze as hard as granite, and then his face relaxed. "Besides, no harm shall come to anyone. It is meant only as a warning to stop their night raids."

"And you think that no one will recognize you and return an eye for an eye?" White Eagle's frustration simmered below the surface of his otherwise calm exterior.

"No one will know from which tribes we come, our faces and horses are painted."

"No one except me." White Eagle reminded him.

"Yes." The great man sighed and scanned the trail ahead of him, then glanced at White Eagle. "I'd hoped you would understand and join us. How could I call up a hunting party and not request the presence of my future blood brother to join us? The council would have been suspicious."

White Eagle gritted his teeth, working the muscles in his jaw. His ears picked up the distant sound of the squeak of wagon wheels. Nausea rose in his throat. So much would change after today. They were no match for white settlers carrying many rifles.

"We are and have always been a peaceful people."

White Eagle grasped Tsula's arm and urged him to stop.

Tsula's gaze traveled from White Eagle's hand slowly to his face. "Wait here. It is only a warning. I will not insist you participate if your conscience tells you not to. My conscience will not let me stand by any longer."

White Eagle knew the rumors of the atrocities that spurned Tsula to his self-imposed mission. He'd heard the stories of the Georgia militia taking on the disciplinary measures themselves, trying to coerce the various tribes to sign up for the emigration lists. Horrible stories of women and children being stripped and beaten for not complying with the emigration requests had filtered back to his clan. While those tribes that did sign the list received food, clothing, and supplies at local stores, maintaining their dignity, at least for the moment. Those who resisted, the followers of Chief Ross scrambled for food in what territory was left by the new settlers.

Chief Ross and his delegation had been in Washington City for many months using government legislative practices to try to gain compliance between the two nations.

This was the information they'd received at the nation's council meetings, yet at what point did each man take the law into his own hands, and at what cost?

White Eagle's gaze clung to Tsula's departing form. As long as they'd known each other, they'd always found the answers to the most difficult questions in using reason.

Perhaps the world in which they now lived was without reason and without the ability to be resolved by reason.

He had seen enough killing in his lifetime. The ghostly impressions came clear as a summer sky into his mind, searing like a firebrand.

His heart pulled tight in his chest at the memory of

his father's last words, as well as seeing his troubled nightmares begin to take shape before his eyes.

"Trust your heart, White Eagle. The Great Spirit will guide you."

A young warrior, barely a man, held his father in his arms as the lifeblood oozed from his wounds.

"Revenge is not the way. It leads to only more bloodshed. Justice will be served, my son," the old man grasped his son's arm, "perhaps not in the same way you think it should."

White Eagle stared at the spot where Tsula disappeared through the trees. He had to find a way to stop this before any more blood was shed.

∞

Sarah shifted, hoping to ease the uncomfortable stiffness radiating up her spine. The morning sun warmed the air, dissipating the thick fog they'd encountered hours before. There had been only one stop earlier, now it was past noon and her stomach reminded her of that fact.

The curtain opened behind her and Laura peered at her with a smile. "Would you mind holding Isabella for a moment? I'd like to tidy up the bedding and she could use some fresh air."

Not at all certain of her abilities with a child, Sarah clumsily took the babe in her arms, grasping the child being thrust at her without warning.

The soft scent of baby skin wafted past Sarah's nose, striking a protective maternal cord within her. She snuggled the gurgling child close to her, tucking the blanket secure around the tiny body. The baby stopped, staring at her with great eyes of china blue.

"Do you mind if I move your hat while I clean?" Laura called from behind the curtain.

"Feel free to toss it to the back. I'm not sure what sort of travel Miss Clara had in mind when she insisted on my wearing it." Not that she wasn't grateful to Miss Clara for the gift, but she preferred her hair down, regardless of how improper it might appear.

"You are a dear little thing," Sarah cooed as she touched a chubby, dimpled fist with her finger. Isabella grabbed it, directing it quickly to her mouth. She stared at her finger, surprised at the strength in the child's suction against her finger. "I think she's hungry." The comment made more to herself than for anyone else.

"I've no doubt. It seems she's never satisfied," Laura's voice issued from behind the curtain. "Offer her your finger for the moment."

Sarah was about to reply to that when the baby whimpered, her face crinkling her displeasure of the lack of sustenance in Sarah's finger. She sought her mind for a way to appease the child.

"Try this." The driver, who'd settled into quiet contemplation long ago, spoke for the first time since morning. He pulled out a lump of raw sugar from his shirt pocket.

Sarah glanced at him dubiously. What could this man possibly know about babies and their needs? "Is it clean?" Sarah raised her chin, eyeing him with skepticism.

"The horses eat it." He shrugged and glanced at the rode. The team fought the reins and for a moment he was distracted with getting them in line.

He nodded toward the sugar. "You got a clean cloth, slip it in there, and twist it. That there will form what they call a teat and the baby will think it's her mama." He chuckled low. "Leastways 'til the sugars gone."

Wary, Sarah pulled out a clean cloth hankie given to her at graduation and wrapped the piece according to the old man's instructions.

The child immediately latched onto the offering, slurping with such satisfied glee, her bird-like lips smacked loudly.

Sarah chuckled, marveling at the result. "She seems content." She smiled at the old man. Then, as if seeing him for the first time, she asked, "What's your name?" Rarely was she open to strangers, particularly men, but with the sun shining bright on this new adventure, she felt less pensive, more curious. Besides, her conversations would make great entries for her journal.

"Gerald, ma'am. Gerald Bixby." He brushed two fingers to the edge of his scruffy felt hat in a greeting befitting a gracious gentleman.

Committing his gesture to memory, Sarah nodded her greeting in response. "It's a pleasure to know you, Mr. Bixby. You seem to know a lot about babies."

"Farmers learn all sorts of tricks like that as they go along. A sugar teat is just one of 'em. We sometimes give them to the runts when they won't suckle with their mamas."

Sarah felt the heat rush to her face.

"Sorry ma'am. I forget that a woman of your stature ain't used to the ways of the farm. I sure didn't mean to offend—"

"Oh no, I…I am familiar with the terminology, Mr. Bixby. In theory, if not in practice." Sarah realized her blushing revealed she had much yet to learn about such things. Perhaps she should not be in such a rush after all, to find a husband.

The old man glanced sideways, giving her a knowing smile, then his gaze riveted ahead. "What the Sam hell—?"

Sarah barely had time to register what happened in the next few moments. Time stood still as one after another of the soldiers in front of the procession toppled off their horses.

Gunfire followed, breaking out sporadically around them, accompanied by wild whooping yells coming at them seemingly from all sides. A moment later, a band of half-naked men on horses came charging at the travelers, their arrows poised in attack.

Sarah instinctively hunched over the child in her lap and watched in surreal horror as the killing spree filtered back toward them.

"Well, not today," Bixby muttered as he pulled back the reins on the team and tried to break from the line. The wagon lurched back, its wheels rolling off the side of the road. The spokes snapped under the strain and the wagon teetered precariously on the steep edge.

Sarah stopped breathing and prayed for a miracle.

A hand grasped the back of the seat and she turned to see Laura's confused expression mixed with fear. "What is happening? The wagon is on the verge of—"

A dark shadow fell across her, hiding the sun from view, and in the next instant Sarah was face-to-face with a fierce look of anger and frustration.

The team reared back at the sound of gunfire as the Indian lunged for the child.

Sarah held tight to Isabella thinking if he could not get the child, he would leave them both. She ducked to a whizzing noise, barely missing her ear and glanced in time to see it make its mark in Bixby's throat. Horrified, no sound came forth from her mouth as she watched his lifeless body keel over the side of the wagon like a sack of grain.

Sarah turned her gaze back to the Indian who now had a solid grasp of her arm. As she held tight to the baby, she flung her jacket at him in attempt to drive him away.

"Come now."

His broken English stunned her long enough that he grabbed her around the waist and hauled her to his horse. She pulled the baby close with little time to ponder the fate of Isabella's mother as the wagon gave a sickening crack and began its descent into the steep ravine.

Certain it would be the final sound she would hear, a woman's loud scream pierced the air and Sarah did not know if it was Laura's or her own.

She squeezed her eyes, trembling inside at what the Indian might do next. Her senses registered a wall of solid, warm male flesh mingled with the scent of the earth. She held tight to Isabella and tried to unscramble her thoughts. Before she could implement the sudden idea of biting her captor, he grabbed her wrist and dropped she and the child to the ground. Sarah opened her eyes and captured his gaze at close range. His expression though stern, held a hint of compassion.

"Hide," he ordered quietly.

The mysterious warrior on his silvery, spotted horse bolted back to toward the wagon train, as her feet stumbled and she began to fall. Hoping to save the child, she tucked her close, twisting her body to receive the first impact. A moment later, her world went black.

Tsula stared in disbelief at the carnage before him. This was not his intent and yet he would be blamed for it. No one was to be hurt and now amidst the entire wagon train lay dozens of Cherokee as well as soldiers. When the great chief of the white people received news of this, there would be justification to step up the terrorist raids. He realized his people now faced the possibility of a more severe retaliation from the settlers.

His head ached, as did his gut. Perhaps though, it was better this way. At least his people would know what they were up against. Perhaps now there would be reason to declare him War Chief.

"I warned you of this," White Eagle called. His voice shook with anger, "Now you have brought a curse upon our people." He yanked his horse's reins as he reached Tsula.

"This was not my plan." Tsula pinned him with an icy stare.

"But it *is* the result, and you alone now must take responsibility." White Eagle twisted to survey the bloody scene, scanning the overturned wagons for the woman and child he'd deposited near the woods. There was no sign of them. With any luck they'd taken their chance to hide. Once it was safe, he would find them and take them to the fort.

"I'm sorry, my brother, but I cannot let this detour me from my duty. No one must know who led this raid, it would destroy other plans already in motion."

Stunned, White Eagle whipped his gaze around in time to feel the searing heat of the arrow drive into the soft flesh of his left shoulder. The force knocked him from his horse and pain like a great fire engulfed his arm. The dull thud of his head meeting solid ground and the pain sparked from it was the last thing he remembered.

CHAPTER FIVE

Angel Woman

The scent of the summer sun warming a meadow of field flowers wafted through his memory aimlessly toying with his ability to reason. Was he in the land of the Great Creator?

White Eagle struggled to open one eye, but the intensity of light shone too bright for his brain to register. He narrowed his gaze, a low moan escaping his lips.

If he were dead, should not all the pain be gone?

"You've been hurt." The voice was gentle as a cloud.

Perhaps he was in the next world after all.

He sensed a delicate hand, its touch like a breeze, renewing the trauma inflicted upon his shoulder. He winced at the flash of pain, grinding his back teeth so as not to scream. Cautiously, he attempted to focus on the angel voice of the Great Beyond.

Instead, he saw a woman, surely of flesh and blood, for she resembled the one he'd dropped at the edge of the woods. His mind struggled to understand how she'd found him, perhaps more why she hadn't left him to die.

His throat was dry, raw from however long he'd laid on the ground. His mind grappled with what to say to her, hoping that his broken English would be discernable through the fatigue beginning to drain his body.

White Eagle had taught himself some of the White man's language, though its alphabet was much more complicated than that of the Cherokee's. The Chief however, encouraged the teachings, especially to the younger tribe's people, so as to bring a greater understanding between the clans and the settlers.

Little good that would do now.

"There is an arrow in your shoulder," the woman spoke in a soft, solemn tone.

White Eagle's gaze was drawn to the compassion in her voice. He glanced at her face, and her eyes gave way her thoughts. She was afraid of him, of what he might do, oddly as he stared up at her from his vulnerable position, he was himself uncertain of what was going on inside him. Fear was not a normal companion for him, particularly in the presence of a beautiful woman.

Her dark hair cascaded over her shoulders and the fierce charge of her green eyes, eyes the color of which he'd never seen before, peered down at him set in a face more beautiful than a summer morning. Perhaps he was hallucinating, for she could easily have been an angel.

Another shard of pain singed the muscle of his shoulder, confirming he was neither dead, nor was she a figment of his imagination. His tongue felt thick, making him curious how long he'd been unconscious. When he tried to speak, the words came out slow and garbled. "How long—?" He coughed, sputtering up a vile taste in his throat. He prayed it wasn't blood.

The sky over her shoulder was a brilliant blue, but the sun no longer shone as brightly overhead. Late afternoon shadows dotted the earth with a dusky, indigo hue.

"Horse," White Eagle managed to croak out in a husky voice he barely recognized as his own.

She straightened, staring down at him from where she

knelt with a mixture of recognition and concern displayed in her face.

In the recesses of his memory he remembered the child and hoped that it had survived. A ragged cry on the ground near his hip gave him his answer.

"Where are we? Can you take me to my father?" She pushed her hands through her hair as though trying to pin it back up the way it had been before he snatched her from the wagon.

He tried to lift his hand, unconsciously wanting to tell her to leave it down. Her image wavered in front of him like an apparition. "Horse," he repeated weakly and hoped none of Tsula's tribesmen remained in the area. He shuddered to think what they might do to the woman and her child.

Her face disappeared like ripples in water as he his strength began to ebb from him. If she could find his horse, he could get them to the Eagle's cave where he could decide how best to get her to the fort, hopefully without incident. Though in the back of his mind, he held little chance of that possibility. Surely they would kill him once they discovered she was from the ambushed wagon train.

The woman stood suddenly, and he attempted to focus his gaze on her movement. Nothing guaranteed that she would not pick up the nearest stone and crack his skull open wide.

She reached to the ground and he braced himself for the inevitable, certain the woman was justified in taking his life. By right of Cherokee code, his people had stolen the lives of many this day in the unprovoked attack.

Instead she pulled the baby into her arms, pausing as

she did to secure the blanket around the child. As a man he could not dismiss the curve of her throat giving way to the swell beneath the white cotton blouse she wore. With her blouse unbuttoned, providing less restraint and her sleeves rolled to her elbows, she gave the appearance of someone not willing to give up.

She stood and he watched her walk away, her hips swaying gently through the tall grass. If she chose, she could find his horse and leave him to die, but something in her eyes caused him to think otherwise.

As a Cherokee, he reprimanded himself for his thoughts of this strange white woman. He quickly averted his gaze, focusing on how to remove the arrow protruding from his body.

Moments clicked by with only the sound of the wind rustling through the tall grass near the edge of the woods. Unknown dangers lived in the grasses and in the surrounding woods, especially after sundown when wild animals came out to feed, preying on the weak and trapped.

From the corner of his eye, he saw a shadow and turned to see the woman walking towards him, holding the reins of the animal in one hand and carrying the pink-blanketed bundle in the other. A dark, red smudge stained the front of her blouse. Perhaps she'd been hurt also. His mind could not remember if the stain had been there before she left or not.

Knowing he needed to get his shoulder patched before he lost more blood, White Eagle curled his fingers firmly around the base of the arrow. Taking several deep breaths, he kept his gaze to hers as she approached.

Her eyes widened as he clenched his jaw, yanking once, wrenching the arrow free. Pain shot through his system and his body stiffened holding in the scream he wanted to release. Finally, his body shuddered and the initial shock lessened, leaving him gasping for air. He knew he hadn't much time to seal off the gaping wound before he bled to death.

He glanced up and found her kneeling once more beside him. This time there was no fear in her eyes, only the look that indicated to him she might be staring at a madman.

"You might have let me get a bandage prepared before you chose to be the almighty brave warrior." She admonished sternly.

Reality played tag with his mind as he pieced together her words. Anger was a good thing, in a sense. It meant she could do what was needed to survive if she had to. Perhaps his initial gut feeling of her being a survivor was indeed true.

She searched the ground around her, and then lay the baby down near him. Without precedence she lifted her skirts and ripped the seam of her undergarment that looked like ruffled riding pants.

In a haze, White Eagle watched in fascination as the material opened revealing a slim white leg.

Pain, emitting fresh from his injury did not afford him the luxury of lingering on her anatomy. "Need yarrow... for the wound." The words struggled from his lips and he grit his teeth holding on to consciousness. White Eagle hoped she could understand that he wanted her to find yarrow and crush it for a pack. The plant would help clot the blood and buy him some time to dress it properly. He prayed he wouldn't bleed to death in the meantime.

He clamped his palm to the sticky wound, his fingers

pressing to keep his lifeblood inside. White Eagle knew if he blacked out again, he might not awaken and then what would happen to her and the child? No, he had to stay alert.

"You want me to find yarrow? You mean the plant?"

He nodded in his weakness, swallowing the bile rising in his throat. Peering at her through one eye, he watched her stand, and then she bent over and picked up his good arm, tucking in the child close at his side. He began to protest, but already she had turned from him, crouching near the underbrush searching for the plant.

The baby whimpered beside him and instinctively he patted the bundle hoping the woman would return soon. If he could save the woman and child, perhaps one senseless act would not have to follow another.

He was not oblivious to the night raids by white settlers. He'd heard the rumors of men with their faces covered by scarves who rode through the Indian communities at night, setting fires, and terrorizing women and children. Yet as bad as those tales, what had happened today was certain to have dire consequences on their people. For that Tsula was to blame.

"I think I have it," she called from a short distance. With an entire yellow plant, roots, and all, held firm in her grasp, she batted away an errant wisp of dark hair and smiled down at him. She was thorough.

Laying it on a flat stone, she took off her shoe and ground the heads of the flower to a coarse pulp. Gathering the clumps into her palms, she nervously raked her teeth over her lip. Only once as she knelt cautiously beside him, did their gazes lock. At that moment he sensed she understood that they needed each other to survive. To his amazement as he watched her, he saw more courage reflected in those luminous eyes than he'd seen in the face of some of his tribesmen.

She placed the pulp on the wound and together with his hand as a guide she pressed the leaves into the wound. She kept her mouth in a fine, tight line as he squeezed his eyes to the pain. When she'd done the best she could do, she reached for the strips of cloth and fashioned a bandage over the wound.

"You need a sling."

She left him momentarily, returning with another blanket and a small leather satchel. Tears stained her pale cheeks and she worked without speaking as she propped his arm in the homemade sling.

"First-aid paid off after all," she muttered and he knew she didn't think he understood.

She was not to blame for the night raids, or for what happened here today. She was an innocent—she and her child.

Intending only to comfort, he lay his hand gently over hers hoping she would see he understood.

Her hand stilled, trembling beneath his and he could see the pulse beating at the base of her throat. She swallowed, averting her gaze from his.

Not wanting to fan the already smoldering fear in her, he removed his hand as carefully as he'd placed it. Only then, did her face relax and she resumed her task. He found her strength and courage admirable, if not attractive and he reminded himself he should not find pleasure in her gentle touch. If he was to protect them both from harm, he had to remain focused and save what energy he had to find them shelter before nightfall.

Sarah sat stoically side-saddle on the stranger's horse, the warmth of his broad chest brushing against her arm at each loping sway of the gray appaloosa. He'd not given her a choice as to where she and Isabella were to ride. Perhaps he needed her body as a prop more than anything. She held the baby close, in some small measure glad that she was alive and able to care for her.

It had been more than Sarah could bear to have to wrench the child's small knapsack from Laura's body. Her heart twisted even now at the realization that Isabella would never know her father or mother. She'd carefully lowered Laura's eyelids saying a prayer for her soul and for their own as she stepped from the wreckage that had hours before been carrying them to a new life.

Her fingers trembled as she took the last of the sugar cubes from Mr. Bixby's pocket, tucking them into her small bag. There was simply no room to carry everything, so she left much of it behind. Isabella's needs were the first priority, her jacket and her journal being the next, hoping she would have the future to use it.

She wasn't sure how long they'd traveled, or where they were destined. The trail led through the woods, twisting and turning as it began a slow ascent toward a low mountain range. They rode in silence, though with each passing moment she wondered what was to become of her and the baby.

His head dropped to her shoulder, startling her for fear he'd died and she shook him until he sat up and studied her with a glazed expression. While logic warned her she had every reason to fear this savage stranger, she also knew that had he intended to harm her, he surely would have done so by now. Perhaps the loss of blood was making him weak—common sense told her that—but more than that she was curious of the warmth in his eyes when he looked at her.

Granted, there were random moments, like when he touched her hand as she dressed his wound that she'd given into her schoolgirl emotions, enjoying his nearness. He was the raw image of passion, greater than any dream of a man she and Emily conjured in their discussions. Maybe it was nothing more than pure fantasy on her part, but there was something oddly protective about being pressed between his arms as they rode. Then again, perhaps her inventive excuses simply placated her deeper fear.

She wondered how best to broach the subject of taking her to the camp. A few days' travel (*surely he knew of the camp?*) and she would see to it that he was adequately compensated for his trouble.

Sarah sensed his gaze before she turned to meet it. His eyes drove deep into her soul, allowing her to see his pride, his concern, and perhaps a tinge of fear as well. They were but a reflection of all that stirred inside of her. Taking a chance, she moistened her lips and spoke, "Camp Sixes, can you take me there?"

He stared blankly at her and for a moment she wondered if he understood, then he shook his head no.

A man of few words, yet apparently he'd understood her. She didn't know whether to be happy or frightened of this revelation.

She cleared her throat, forcing calm into her voice, "Why?" Her brows knit with inquiry and she turned to face him better, hoping her aggressive behavior might change his mind.

His gaze narrowed on her and he frowned holding a steady gaze which she was sure was designed to intimidate.

It worked…almost.

His frown was nearly as frustrating as his refusal to take her to where she wished to go. Though probably unwise, impatience persisted inside her. Those that knew her had often praised her for her tenacity and logical thinking. She was known among her friends and classmates as having great organizational skills. Thus, armed with this knowledge, she hoped to help him see reason.

She tapped her chest with the palm of her hand, staring intently into his indifferent gaze. "You take—" She pointed to Isabella. "Baby and me to white man's fort. Camp Sixes."

She blinked ignoring what she thought might be a glint of mischief in his dark eyes. Was that a smile curling at the corner of his mouth? Shaking off the silly notion that he knew perfectly well what she was asking, she quirked her brow.

He did the same, and then averted his attention to the trail ahead.

Clearly the man was stubborn, not unlike his white male counterparts, ignorant in thinking that women were best when silent. Frustrated with her predicament, she stared dumbly at the base of his throat. His features from the tip of his nose to the deerskin moccasins on his feet were as hard as granite. His hair shone long and black in the diminishing rays of the sun. Her gaze lowered to his span of muscled chest, gleaming bronze in the twilight. Try as she might to imagine him in a civilized man's wardrobe, the shaky image would not permit the same fierce magnificence as what she observed at close range. Blowing out a dejected sigh, she glanced at his firm jaw, and then focused on Isabella resting in her arms. *What would her future be? What kind of man would Isabella choose one day to marry?* Did this Indian think that Isabella was hers? Was that the reason he saved them? Did he *now* think he had a ready-made family? Disturbing as the idea might be, a tingles raced over her skin. She glanced at his stoic face and considered what he might do if he knew the truth-that the baby was not hers. Perhaps it was wiser to let him think so for now. When he was on the mend from his wound and both were rested, then she would explain and reason with him.

CHAPTER SIX

Far from Home

The sky was darkening by the time she felt the warrior tug on the reins and halt the horse. Deep shadows blanketed the steep hillside. Sarah could barely discern the terrain underfoot. Why had he stopped in such a dangerous place? She had to keep her wits about her. Scanning the area, she determined that had he wanted her dead, they would be, leaving a host of other possibilities twisting in her mind.

Her rescuer slipped off the horse, stumbling as he reached the ground.

Sarah clutched the horse's mane, debating her chances of survival if she rode off now, or to stay with him and face what may come.

He braced himself against a large boulder and reached his arms out toward her.

For a scant moment, she was stunned by his gesture, then quickly realized it was meant for the baby and not for her.

Isabella slept content, wrapped snug in her pink and yellow patchwork quilt, exhausted by the days' events and lulled by the gentle sway of the ride.

Her reason warred with trust as she held out the child to him.

The Indian held her gaze as he gathered the child close, tucking the blanket around her as carefully as any father.

He then turned and began to climb the trail that was protected by a cluster of trees.

His paternal gesture, so caring and thoughtful touched something deep in Sarah, though she wasn't sure it was proper to entertain such ideas.

It registered suddenly that he'd taken Isabella and was disappearing from view into the wooded shadows. Grabbing the satchel, she slid quickly from the horse uncertain if she should tie the reins somewhere, or leave him there.

"Stay," she declared the edict unsure of what else to do, and then grabbed her skirt hem and scurried in the direction of the man who had Isabella. What was she thinking? She'd been better off to ram her heels to the horse's side and search for a settler's camp when she'd had the chance.

Twigs scraped at her ankles as she stepped over and around the boulders that lay in the path. Ahead, she could see his massive form silhouetted against the evening sky. Blinking once to clear out a piece of grit in her eye, she reopened them and he was gone. He and Isabella had vanished completely!

Frantically searching the path, fear climbed high into her throat. Solid rock loomed to her left and a wooded drop-off to her right. She squinted to see if they'd fallen over the edge, but heard nothing. Nausea churned in her stomach and she turned not thinking the child would not understand her and cupped her hands to her mouth, "Isabella!" Her mind scattered and reason fell apart at the seams.

In the inky darkness, something reached out catching hold of her skirt and she screamed as she fell to her knees. The next thing she knew she was being dragged into a small opening in a cave. Her eyes could not focus in the dark, but her body knew it was the Indian. She could hear Isabella's gurgling coos.

"Sleep here."

Cramped tightly in the narrow cave entrance, she felt the heat of his breath on her face as he spoke. Relieved, afraid, and overwhelmed with gratitude for his gentle nature, as well as their blind intimacy she pressed forward in the dark finding his face with her hands. She could hear his labored breathing and felt the muscle in his jaw clench beneath her fingers.

"Thank you, "she whispered, and then, meaning only to kiss his cheek, accidentally touched her lips to his. She hadn't intended for it to happen. Terrified at what he might think—what he might do, she backed away, bumping soundly against the rock wall. "I'm sorry; it's been a horrid day. I—"

The words stopped in her throat as his fingers brushed deftly across her cheek. Fatigue should not give way to arousal, logically she knew, but at that moment she wished for nothing more than to be held in his great protective arms.

As suddenly as the thoughts appeared they dissipated as she realized he was moving past her and further into the cave. Following close, a chill snaked up her arms and she hoped the quilt would be enough for Isabella. In the next moment, a current of air swept beneath the hem of her skirt and she realized she could stand upright.

"I hope there are no bats," she muttered.

She heard a rustling of his feet to the earth floor and then Isabella was stuffed back into her arms.

From a small opening high above them, she could detect the faint light of the waning sun. At her feet, the clack of stones being hit together piqued her curiosity. She stared at his huddled form in the semi-darkness and then she smelled smoke.

In an instant, a small spark ignited, setting a small patch of straw on fire, it shed a modest illumination on the walls of the cave dwelling.

Brushing away her skirts from the flame, she looked about her, checking her surroundings. At some point, it would appear that this was someone's dwelling, perhaps used by hunters, or perhaps her captor? Most importantly, it was shelter, warm and dry from animals and the elements.

Was he her savior? Confused by many things and plagued by fatigue, she searched the shallow edge of rock and sat down. She tucked her skirts in around her feet, and huddled close to the wall holding Isabella close.

With his dark hair tied back with a strip of leather, he continued to work the fire, gently blowing across the flames. It appeared the least of his concerns was to advise her of his plans, and truth was, she wasn't sure she wanted to know just yet.

Instead she sat silent, thinking of her sedate life of not quite twenty-four hours' past. Thoughts of Emily setting the table in the dining hall for the evening meal, of girlish laughter echoing in the house, deciding which ribbon to wear with her ball gown for the annual Christmas cotillion.

All faded, replaced by the stark reality of the man before her. New York and Miss Emma's Boarding school were a million miles away.

A tear escaped, trailing down her cheek and she swiped it away in frustration. The gesture woke Isabella and she cursed mentally of thinking only of herself. Her other senses advised her of the child's other needs as well as that of her apparent hunger. Fortunately, the satchel; had several clean cloths packed for the journey, but she knew at some point, given how long they would be detained from reaching the fort that she would have to wash the soiled cloth in a stream.

The sudden vivid memory of Laura's vacant blue gaze staring at her reinstated the sorrow twisting her heart, but also it fanned the flame of determination that she alone would have to find a way to care for Isabella. If it was the last task she had on this earth.

"I will need water for the child." Her words spoken with more boldness than she'd intended, ricocheted off the walls of the small stone room. She eased her back to the wall behind her, gripping Isabella tighter.

He glanced up at her with the stoic gaze she was fast becoming used to.

"Water?" she mouthed enunciating each syllable.

He stared at her as though contemplating how to answer.

"Wa—"

"Water. For the child, yes?" His dark gaze held her surprised one.

Sarah's jaw slacked open. The savage understood her? Why hadn't he answered earlier?

"I will need water to cleanse this wound." He glanced at his shoulder.

"You speak English? All this time you made me think you were a—" Sarah's ire rose.

"A savage?"

She blushed as he spoke the very word she'd used in

her mind more than once.

"But—"

"No time. I must get water for your child." He reached forward, smoothing Isabella's curly ringlets with two long fingers of a powerful looking hand.

She noted he possessed the strong hands of a hunter, a capable warrior, hands that had character—life. Sarah pushed the direction of her thoughts away and focused on Isabella. "I'm not really—" Sarah's confession halted as his dark gaze met hers. She knew it was best she should tell him the true identity of Isabella's mother, yet part of her cautioned being to open with the stranger, no matter how compassionate his manner.

He waited with patience, the intensity of his gaze rattling her every nerve, penetrating her thoughts, making her think he possessed the ability to look right through her.

She shivered.

He stood, bracing his hand to the wall to steady himself.

"Feed the child. I will return soon." He paused, frowning as he tipped his head studying her with great interest.

She realized his gaze scrutinized her breasts and she pulled in her shoulders preventing his view.

"Are you dry?"

Startled by his bluntness, she stared at him with wide eyes. She had no idea men knew of such things. "Am I what?" Her mouth went dry.

"Your milk."

Her mouth slacked open, yet she could not speak even if she could think of what to say.

Before she could object, he knelt to one knee and

gingerly lifted one breast and then the other, as though weighing their content. She sat in humiliated horror gazing at those same hands she'd admired moments before fondling her like a piece of meat in a market. Sweat broke out on her forehead as he eyed her with great concern. She raised her hand to bat him away.

He sat back on his heels. "I have seen this happen." He nodded, still staring at her breasts. "The milk will return with proper rest and food. Mother Earth takes pleasure in the gift offerings of a mother to her child."

A multitude of emotions invaded her senses as she stared into his face. Her brain grappled with his unsolicited instruction on motherhood, while struggling with the reality that no man had ever touched her intimately before.

Apparently this was not the case for him as he awaited expectantly her answer.

"I, uh—" The words clogged her throat as much as the sensations of his intimacy with her body fogged her brain.

He frowned again and left through the narrow opening without another word.

Leave now! She should take advantage of this time and escape. What other freedoms would this man impose on her before she could find a way to convince him to take them to the camp?

Sarah glanced through the small hole, watching the steady curl of smoke escape to the sky. Beyond she could see the sprinkling of brilliant stars. Yet even their brilliance would not be enough to effectively guide her way through the unknown woods. For the moment it appeared she would have to stay where she was, if not only for the sake of the child. She prayed she would know what to do in the event he should try to take advantage of her.

Her mind raced, as did her heart to dwell on such things, so she twisted another lump of sugar in her hankie and offered the confection to Isabella. The babe greedily accepted it, gurgling and cooing with contentment. She changed her cloth and rewrapped her in the blankets, then lay down on the bed of straw and drew her close in the crook of her arm, shielding her from the fire.

Sarah dozed, waking to each sound she heard. Once she thought a wolf or fox might be entering the cave, but it turned out to be a small gray squirrel that darted in scratching frantically for a stash of walnuts behind a pile of stones. After the animal left, Sarah pulled off her jacket and fashioned a pallet for Isabella. Then she went in search of the nuts. Once found she took several and placed them on the flat stone floor and smashed them open with a rock.

"Good. You will need your strength."

Her heart stopped at the deep voice behind her. She turned; cheeks filled with nuts and stared at him. She'd not heard him return. Chewing quickly, she swallowed, painfully forcing down the half-chewed food.

"What do your people call you?"

"My people…uh, my name is Sarah." She eyed the gourd dangling from his hand, hoping it was water. Her greed in forcing too many walnuts in her mouth had all but dried her throat. Certainly it was not the flicker of humor in his knowing gaze that caused her parched discomfort.

"I am White Eagle." He dropped the cloth sack and gourd to the floor, and Sarah caught the slight wince in his breath.

"I don't suppose there is water in that urn?" Sarah recognized and was slightly embarrassed at the aristocratic tone in her voice. It did not go unnoticed by her half-naked companion either.

His brow arched. "Has the child eaten then?" he spoke as he handed her the gourd, "drink here." He tapped the small hole with his index finger.

Though she was besieged with guilt, she knew she'd done the best she could for Isabella, at least for the moment. "Um, yes, she ate quite well." It wasn't a complete lie.

He nodded as if accepting her story as truth. It didn't help her guilt any.

"We must stay here until the sun rises again, then we will follow the path to the white man's camp." He dropped to his knees near the fire, adding a few twigs of straw to the dwindling flames. Drawing an apple from the bag, he looked at Sarah.

"Why must we wait? Can't we go tonight?" Her gaze dropped to the fruit in his hand and she eyed it hungrily.

Swiping it once over his deerskin loincloth, he held out the apple to her. Questions of why they could not continue their journey while it was still dark flitted vaguely in her mind, but the draw of the sweet, red apple in his hand held her attention.

He pressed it toward her. "Eat. Get your strength."

She hesitated as images of her biblical upbringing and the story of Adam and Eve dancing in her head.

"Take. Eat." He prodded.

"What will you eat?" She glanced at his wound. Soon it would need to be redressed. Who was this man that risked his life to protect a white woman and her baby?

Sarah averted her gaze from his, certain that he would

see the questions in her eyes.

He ignored her question, dropping the apple into her open palm.

Her body tingled as the tips of his fingers brushed across her palm in the process. Everything outward about this man appeared strong and solid, unapproachable, but his manner, his gentleness she found odd. Though it pleased her in ways she didn't think it would.

"Your wound? Is there a great deal of damage?" Her gaze dropped to the sheen of the firelight flickering on his sinewy bronze shoulder. In the shadows cast by the fire and the extent of her fatigue, his sheer physical strength was magnified.

Sarah's thoughts tripped back to the sensation of his gentle touch, so careful and thorough in their investigation. She cleared her throat, dismissing how her body tensed just thinking about it. With a quick detour to thoughts of food, she bit solidly into the apple and chose to glance up at the hole in the cave ceiling, rather than meet his gaze. Realizing she had not gone to the bathroom in hours, the urge to do so was suddenly overwhelming.

"Um, I need to use…" She'd started to say the outhouse, and then realized her mistake. "I'll be just a minute." She stood, as did he. Cautiously, she stepped around him, careful not to let their bodies touch, she bent to retrieve the child.

"The child is safe." He placed his hand on her arm.

Torn between need and with having to make a judgment on his sincerity, Sarah decided she had little choice.

"There is a river, if you wish to bathe. Though your eyes should be keen for night animals." His gaze captured hers and she swore a glint of challenge flitted across his eyes.

"Thank you." She glanced at his wound.

"It is deep, but the bleeding has stopped."

It registered he had answered her question. She gave him a weak smile and nodded.

"The child sleeps in peace." He glanced at Isabella, and then cast his gaze on her. "No doubt a full belly."

Sarah refused to look again in his eyes for she suspected he would see the truth of her deception. Lifting her skirts above her ankles, she turned toward the opening. "If you'll excuse me, I'm going to step outside."

"Do not wander far, Sarah."

She paused, checking once over her shoulder and caught his steady gaze through the heat of the campfire. His eyes sparkled like black river rock in the dim light. So mesmerized that she hadn't realized she was staring until he tipped his head with a questioning look.

"Your eyes are the color of a green meadow in summer, Sarah."

She vaguely heard the words, but she blinked at them in disbelief. Had this Cherokee just paid her a compliment? No one that she could remember had ever given her one with such simple sincerity. She wasn't at all sure how it should cause her to feel or that it should create any feelings at al—but it did. Rather than broach what skittered in her mind, she swallowed, turned, and walked directly into the low-hanging stone in front of her. She stumbled back and landed with un-ladylike grace on her backside.

White Eagle was beside her before she realized what happened. "Crouch low when you leave." He took her chin between his fingers and studied her face, turning it to the left and then the right. "It is a small wound. It should be well by the morning light."

He offered then an easy smile that had greater impact on her than that of the rock. She was grateful to already be sitting, as she wasn't sure her legs would have carried her.

"Do you wish me to follow?" He narrowed his concerned gaze searching her face.

"No." Sarah regained her mental processes. "That won't be necessary. I'm sure I'll manage…fine." She scrambled up, ignoring her delicate skin scraping on the rocky floor and gathered her skirts. Suddenly something large and firm landed on top of her head. Sarah turned to his stoic face as he pushed her head down and she waddled through the opening.

Her first time alone with a man and already she'd managed to lie, humiliate herself, be touched intimately by him, and kiss the stranger, all in the same night.

Her father would have a fit.

Sarah grinned impishly as she stepped into the moonlight.

∞

White Eagle stared at the woman's silhouette shaped by the swathe of moonlight. He could not help but wonder how long she'd been married before producing this child, or where her husband was at this moment? Was he killed in the attack? Or was he waiting for her at one of the white men's camps? Her manner around him suggested she was innocent to the ways of a man and yet she had a child. The idea when presented in his mind gave way to more confusion than he needed at the moment.

He glanced at the sleeping child. What custom of her

people permitted kissing another man while belonging to another?

White Eagle shook his head in puzzlement, and then settled himself on the floor. A fresh jolt of pain shot through his system and he knew that he should have taken the time to cleanse his wound more thoroughly. It was all he could do to sneak into his village unnoticed, gather a few items, and speak to Running Doe quickly without being noticed. He could not chance that anyone would see him and tell Tsula that he was alive. Better that he should consider him dead.

"What shall I do, my brother?" Running Doe stuffed dried deer meat into the bag, working quickly as she spoke.

"Pack up what you need, the old men and women will need to ride, the rest can walk. Take them to the hills, into the caves and stay there. We do not know how long we will have to stay. Soon it will not be safe to stay here." White Eagle pressed a palm to his shoulder.

"Let me dress your wound." His sister held out her hand to him, but he shook his head.

"There is no time. You must tell the elders. You must leave before the sun rises." He grabbed her upper arm forcing her to look at him. "Promise you will do this."

"I trust you, White Eagle. This is what you have seen in your night visions, is it not?"

He stared at his sister weighing her ability to grasp all he had seen in his dreams. It was best for now, that she simply trust, and follow his instruction. There would be time for greater explanation later, when they were all safe. He nodded. That would be all she needed for now.

"Where is your camp?"

"In the cave below the Eagle's Nest."

"Three of you in that small cave? There was barely room for the two of us as children." Running Doe's eyes held a curious sheen. "This white woman, is she pretty?"

Keeping his expression bland as he could, White Eagle shrugged. "She is a white woman with a child." Something like a bad turnip caused his stomach to churn and he pushed away the scent of her skin in his mind.

"And when do you plan to take her and the child to the white camp, my brother?" She handed him the deerskin knapsack, arching her brow in question.

"When it is safe to do so." He grasped the neck of the sack, and then turned to leave.

"Be careful, White Eagle. You will come to us soon?"

"I will meet you." He closed his eyes briefly, quelling the nausea rising in his throat. His vision blurred momentarily.

"White Eagle? You are not well—"

His sister's hand touched his arm and his eyes flew open. "I must get back. It will be well, my sister." He hoped he would stay alert enough to get back to the cave. By now, Sarah will have wondered if he would return, or perhaps she decided to try to find the camp herself, alone, in the dark. White Eagle gripped the bag tighter, forcing what energy he had left into focusing on his sister. "I will meet you soon."

CHAPTER SEVEN

Guardian Stranger

Fatigue swarmed White Eagle's senses and he closed his eyes, wishing she would return so he could rest. He'd narrowly escaped being seen by Tsula and his followers on the way back from the village. He knew that he would need to find a way to get the woman and her child to their camp very soon, before Tsula discovered he harbored a survivor of the attack. Another wave of nausea swept over White Eagle and he swallowed the bile in his throat. Now all he had to do was to live long enough to get her there.

His thoughts drifted in and out of broken scenes of the day, trying to determine if there was anything more he could have done. Tsula and his men had set themselves up as the keepers of the law of balance. For all the death and ill-will the new white settlers brought upon the previous tribes of Cherokee, those who journeyed into Cherokee territory must now take responsibility for those deeds. True the white men had made practice of terrorizing the villages, specifically women and children during night raids, but Tsula had since taken on the soul duty of retaliation.

He knew the woman's scent before she entered into the cave's main chamber, but his eyes heavy with sleep would not afford him the strength to look at her. He folded his hands over his chest and yawned.

"What shall I do with the fire?" she whispered.

She was a woman who thought less of herself and for that she had his admiration.

"It will die out on its own."

"Do you need anything?" Her voice was closer now; it's sound like a soft breeze on a summer afternoon. A chill skated across his flesh, knowing that such a statement given by a Cherokee woman would guarantee her another good number of hours of a man's attention.

He turned his head, forcing his eyes open and caught her concerned gaze. White women were peculiar he decided—beautiful, at least this one—but peculiar just the same. She had no concept of what she offered.

"You should sleep."

"I've every intention to do so, Mr. White Eagle." She sat back on her heels and stared at him, those large green eyes making his thoughts feel exposed. Perhaps she was not as innocent as he'd thought.

"This is good. You will need rest for the journey." A mix of emotions flitted through her gaze before she brushed at the cave floor and lay down. Keeping her gaze steady on his, she drew the child close to her breast.

"The child is warm?" His gaze skipped past the odd look in the woman's eyes and rested on the quiet bundle huddled close to her.

She frowned as she stared at him through the receding firelight. "Will we be traveling with your people tomorrow?"

So she was assertive as well, intriguing given that he'd been led to believe that white women were weak and for the most part helpless. She was not unlike Running Doe in many ways. He could be as stubborn. A spark of amusement skittered across his heart.

"The child?" He calmly reiterated.

"She is quite warm; I assure you," she paused, "and my question, please?"

White Eagle closed his eyes and breathed deep. If all went well, his people would be well on their way to safety and he would be on his way to the camp with Sarah and the child. On a good day his sister's persistence tested his patience. This woman walked on hot coals given his fatigue and the fact that his shoulder burned like a hot ember. "No, this is your answer." He hoped his firm tone would quell further questioning, his body screamed for sleep.

"And why not?"

Running Doe could learn much from this woman's tenacity. "I must find a way to take you to the camp you seek. Your people will be watching for your arrival." He knew if it were him waiting for her arrival, he would be searching the trails for her even now. The thought was a dangerous one, he knew. Too much familiarity with this woman was not wise. He would do well to keep his emotions stowed away, saved for a Cherokee woman that would one day choose him as her husband.

"Perhaps not if word has reached the fort about the attack of your people." She leaned up on her elbow, blatantly challenging him. Her husband may yet lay lifeless on the road and yet this woman acted as though she thought little of it. Curious to know more about her and the child, it was fortunate that his body required more rest than he had energy to pursue the truth. Perhaps less knowledge was better in this instance.

"Rest now. Tomorrow will come soon and we will make plans." He shifted, wincing as a sharp pain flashed through his shoulder.

"Here." She held out her small satchel to him. "Place this beneath your shoulder for support."

Moved by her kindness, he reached for the bag, following her instructions. Remarkably the pressure on his shoulder eased. He shut his eyes, frowning as the memory of the day filtered through his thoughts. As gentle as her recent gesture, her kiss of unplanned gratitude entered his dreams, and he drifted peacefully into sleep.

Sarah watched him, unable to sleep for her thoughts. Glad for the time alone to think about her situation, she observed the steady rise and fall of his chest and contemplated what his world was like.

She pulled her journal from the deep pocket of her traveling skirt and flipped through until she found a blank page. Touching the pencil nib deftly to the tip of her tongue, she scribbled in the small book.

Perhaps by now news of the ambush has reached the fort. It is my hope that our soldiers and the settlers living nearby will not retaliate against the innocent tribes who had no part in the horrible attack.

Sarah paused, glancing at the man sleeping soundly before her. What had been his role in the attack? What plans did he truly have for her and Isabella? He'd mentioned taking her to the camp, but how would he be able to accomplish that task without endangering himself? Sarah was certain if news of the attack had indeed reached the fort, the military would capture and perhaps torture him the minute he stepped into the compound. What reason would he have for putting himself in such a position?

Her gaze roamed lazily over his form, at first deep in thought, but soon she found herself mentally noting things once curious to her. Innocent in many ways, she'd not gazed upon flesh save that her own, much less that of a half-naked sleeping man.

Sarah swallowed against the sensation of her body's awareness to the handsome warrior. He stirred emotions in her yet untried, this quiet man born in a world she knew nothing about.

Her gaze stopped at his mouth parted slightly in his slumber. She touched her fingers to her lips remembering the textured contrast of his. The desire to capture this moment for the sake of her memory quickened inside and she flipped to a clean page and began to sketch the ruggedly attractive man. With each stroke she recreated his image on paper, her pencil capturing each detail until she realized the frenzied pace of her work matched that of her heart. Embarrassed at the lack of control of her emotions, Sarah reasoned that much of it could be attributed to fatigue, aided no doubt by her situation. Of course, that was it.

She tamped down her runaway feelings and finished her closing entry.

What comes with the dawn remains a mystery. I fear no harm from this man to either myself or little Isabella. Is this the adventure Emily pre-ordained I would have? Still, I cannot overlook the opportunity to study this breed of people who have lived on this land for generations. Certainly, long before English speaking settlers arrived seeking gold in the rivers and hills. How much I could learn from him and in turn, teach to my students and perhaps help quell the misconceptions about the Cherokee.

She looked at White Eagle and wondered what misconceptions he had of the white man, or for that matter, white women? Pushing away the unknown emotions curling deep inside her, she continued.

I fear he still believes the child is mine, though by now he surely wonders why I have not spoken of a husband. Perhaps to have a child out of wedlock is more common among his people? Perhaps though, he believes he has some sort of ownership since we are under his care.

The hair on Sarah's neck prickled at the thought. Miss Emma had taught her pupils clearly that women were not possessions and indeed in many ways were just as capable of many things men could achieve. A flicker of a thought danced merrily across the shadows of her present dilemma. What would it be like to be married to such a man? Did Indians have many wives? For all her education of books and classroom, there was little she knew about the real world, much less that of the Cherokee. Flicking away her silly musings with a quick shake of her head, she wrote.

Certainly such an idea would and should be quickly dispelled as ridiculous and frivolous. Our lives are strange to one another, our customs foreign, and our education on completely different levels, his in the wild and mine in the classroom. When one gets to the crux of the matter all we really have in terms of a would-be commonality for marriage is that he is a man, and I am a—

Sarah's fingers fumbled with the pencil as she sensed the heat of a blush in her face. With firm resolve, and even a firmer grip on her writing utensil, she finished her entry.

A woman.

The lead broke with the forced punctuation she contributed to the sentence and she slammed the book so as not to face again what her own hand had wrought. Warning bells rang soundly in her head.

"Nothing except that he is a man and I am a woman."

The very concept sounded so primitive, yet as equally enticing to that part of her yet curious on such matters. She stuffed the journal in her skirt pocket and lay down quickly on the cold, hard floor, adjusting her jacket sleeve over Isabella's tiny body.

With her gaze fixed on the flames leaping in the fire, she watched them fade into her dreams.

The scent of cooking meat roused Sarah from her slumber. For a moment, before it registered to her where she was, it triggered a memory of boarding school on cold mornings when Ms. Clara would prepare sausages for the morning meal.

She stretched, at once realizing she was not at school, nor was it fragrant meat creating the scent tickling her nose. Following the smell, she turned her head to see the edge of her leather satchel beneath White Eagle's shoulder smoldering in the fire's embers. Scrambling from the floor, she grabbed her shoe and beat at the strap, pushing it away from the smoking fire. At the same time confused as to why White Eagle continued to sleep so soundly.

Isabella awoke and Sarah knew she would be hungry, and in need of changing. When the young child stuffed her tiny fist into her mouth and began to wail, Sarah glanced worriedly toward White Eagle, yet he slept as though he were alone. If she could get him away from the cave, perhaps she could coerce Isabella with another sugar cube to quell her appetite.

Sarah's guilt drew her gaze to the infant. She knew she would need proper sustenance and soon. Perhaps it would be best to come forth and tell the man her truth?

She picked up Isabella, placing her ring finger in her mouth hoping to appease her for a moment while she thought of a plausible explanation. Seeing no other way around her dilemma, she swallowed hard and touched his shoulder, being careful not to startle him, as she wasn't sure of his reflexes.

His skin however, felt clammy to the touch and chilled. For an instant she feared he was dead. She glanced at his shoulder still wrapped in the improper dressing she'd administered the morning before. How could she have not noticed that it had not been changed? Had his blood loss been too much to survive?

"Mr. White Eagle?" She fought back the panic in her voice, ignoring the squirming child in her arms. "Wake up!" Closing her eyes, she took a deep breath and laid her head to his chest. Though weak, a heartbeat still thrummed slowly. Rising to search his face, she placed her palm to his forehead and felt then the heat of his fever.

White Eagle turned his head, pulling away from her touch and moaned something she could not decipher.

Despite her persistent wailing of her discomfort, Sarah quickly placed Isabella on the pallet bed and turned back to White Eagle, cradling his face between her hands.

"No." His face was taut, straining against his fever.

"I cannot lose you." She realized with crystalline clarity the truth of her words. If he should die, what would become of them? How long would they wander until someone found them, whether it was white settlers, renegade Indians, or wild animals? The thought set off a fresh wave of fear inside her.

She grasped his face in one hand and shook him until his eyes fluttered open. "Don't you dare take us captive and then abandon us to those savages." The fierce tone in her voice garnered his attention, weak though it was.

He grabbed her wrist preventing her from taking her panic out on him. "Go—outside. Bring sumac berries and leaves. Make tea with water. The tea will—" He held tight her wrist, his gaze narrowing as if trying to focus.

"Will what? Where can I find these berries?" She broke free of his grasp and gently patted his firm cheek.

"Out—near the mountainside." His head listed to one side as he slipped back into his delirium.

"What shall I boil tea in?" She spoke aloud as she stood, turning in circles trying to assess what she needed to do. Pressing her palms to her temples, she forced herself to stop and think logically. First, she would need to get the fire going strong again. She glanced at Isabella who lay silent staring up at her, apparently more enthralled at Sarah's manner than her own hunger.

Dropping to her knees, she bent low over the warm ashes as she'd seen him do earlier. Blowing gently over the top of the glowing embers, she received a face full of gray ash twice, before a thin plume of smoke lifted from the charred depths. She tucked a few bits of straw over the smoke, pleased when she saw a tiny flame come to life.

Scooping Isabella into her arms, she headed toward the cave entrance. If his horse waited outside, there would be nothing to prevent her from taking it and following the river until she came upon a white settler's camp. The idea flitted through her mind, carefully rounding upon the concept that White Eagle had saved her and Isabella from certain death. To what end, she still did not know, but perhaps she owed him as much.

Stepping into the brilliant sunshine of early morning

she spied his horse, and then saw the brilliant red of a sumac bush in its burnished glory. She paused briefly to weigh her options. At the base of a tree lay a gnarled branch that would serve perhaps to hold the gourd of water over the fire. From her small brush with simple emergency training—Miss Emma insisted each of her pupils knew at least the basics—she remembered certain varieties of sumac were indeed poisonous when ingested. How could she be sure this was the correct variety? *He* had been the one to point it out to her, she reasoned in silence, all the while studying his horse leisurely nipping away at a clump of grass.

Her conscience led her next steps as she gathered sumac leaves and berries stuffing them in her skirts lifted to form a pouch. If she could tear away the strap of her leather satchel it might provide the means for hanging the gourd over the fire.

She blew an errant wisp of hair from her face as she grappled with Isabella in one hand and the balancing the berries in the other. Adrenaline pumped in her system, as the sun rose higher in the sky. Sweat trickled between her breasts, sliding down her spine as she worked fast as she could with one hand. The sudden chirping of a group of sparrows through the silent forest fanned the possibility that without her help, he could die. The thought heightened her awareness of how at this very moment she and Isabella were vulnerable to the unknown dangers of the forest. She quickened her pace, ignoring the stinging barbs of the bush.

A few moments later, Sarah's attention jumped back and forth from the blackening bottom of the gourd to the muted moans coming from White Eagle. Uncertain as to exact portions, she simply used her experience back at school in making Earl Grey tea and prayed she was close to what was needed. A small mixture of sugar and water had done well toward satisfying Isabella along with a change of a clean under cloth. She now lay asleep on the crude pallet, oblivious to a man's life hanging in the balance and at the very hands of the woman who cared for her.

Sarah stared through weariness at the small form of the child, renewing her urgent determination to make White Eagle well.

She carefully lifted the gourd from the fire, using her skirt as a pad from the heat and sat it atop three small stones set to hold the round-bottomed container. Taking her handkerchief, she wrapped a small portion of the crushed mountain leaves and berries within and tied it tight. Attaching it to a small stick, she doused the bag up and down, steeping it in the boiled water. The scent of the tea-like concoction permeated the air with an earthy aroma and she hoped they would not be overcome with vapors.

Her next dilemma was in how to feed him the drink. She scanned the cave, her eyes lighting on the stash of walnuts made by the squirrel. Finding an unmarred half-shell, she hollowed its center with a stick and smoothed it with her finger, hoping no residue would affect the purpose of the tea.

With precision steadiness, she dipped the walnut shell into the warm liquid and scooted to White Eagle's side. "Sip this. I did as you asked. Please, please wake up."

Unable to stir him, she dropped the shell and poked her finger into the steamy concoction.

Lifting his head slightly, she ran her finger slowly over his bottom lip. She waited for his response, his fever still burned, and she feared all was for naught. Ripping her blouse at its shoulder seam, she yanked it from her arm and dipped a twisted end into the medicine. Her heart pounding, afraid she might be too late; she placed her fingers near his mouth and forced it open. Slowly the drops of the sumac tea fell into his mouth, one, two, and then three. She lifted the cloth away and let his headrest on the cave floor. Sarah hoped against the odds that he would recover, but she would not deny the possibility. If she had to, she would take Isabella and they would take their chances getting to the camp.

"Please. We need you." Her fingers deftly brushed over his chest and her heart lurched with the strength she sensed beneath her hand. Lifting a strand of hair from his face, she noticed a large bruise near his hairline. Odd that she'd not seen that until now. Peering closer, she tried to make out the severity of the wound. Perhaps she could find more yarrow and redress his shoulder while he was still.

"Running Doe—" White Eagle muttered in his delirium. His hand sought hers.

Something about the way he called the name made her curious as to whom she was. There was gentleness in his voice and though, due in part to his illness, Sarah could tell there was soft admiration for the woman's name. Perhaps it was his wife? More surprising was the stab of jealousy that followed her thoughts.

Shaking away her imbecilic behavior, she wondered if he would remember her name. "It is me, Mr. White Eagle. Sarah."

Shifting closer, she placed her arm beneath his head, resting it on her lap. She dipped the hollow walnut shell in the tea, positioning his head so he could sip from it. This time, his lips moved marginally to accommodate her efforts. Sip after sip he struggled, some escaping the corners of his mouth, dampening her skirts.

"You must try. You must get well," she whispered softly.

With one last sigh, he slid lifeless from her grasp.

Was he dead? Had he fallen into unconsciousness? Sarah dabbed at the corners of his mouth, and placed two fingers at the side of his neck. Thankfully there was a strong pulse. Now all she could do was to wait and see if this strange remedy would heal.

After cleaning him up, she brewed a fresh batch of the mountain medicine, steeping the leaves through her small hankie as though preparing tea for the afternoon. Much of her time however, was spent sitting with his head in her lap, soothing his brow, and willing him to recover.

What would her papa say to see her now? Would he understand her basic need to care for the injured or would he see her efforts as a foolish waste of time? In her silence, she fought to remember her father and his views. He very rarely discussed business or political matters around her, his manner most generally made her feel as though he patted her on the head for being the dutiful daughter.

It was Emily's influence that had brought her out of the shell her father had placed her in. Emily, her wild and rebellious friend, would give her right arm for the adventure she was having.

"There is more out there, Sarah than these four walls allow. Much to see and even more to experience," Emily had said with a sly smile. She often wondered how her friend knew so much about the outside world, but she also knew how resourceful Emily could be when she wanted to be.

Such thoughts frightened her at first, but as Sarah grew, so did her relationship with Emily. She began to have vivid dreams and journal her thoughts privately in her diaries. As of late, her dreams included the dark silhouette of a man, built like a great tree in the forest. She never saw his face, nor did she know whether his intent was toward good or harm, but each time she dreamt of him, she would awaken the next morning with a cold sweat.

Sarah glanced down at White Eagle's sleeping face. Was there really much to fear from this man other than the color of his skin or the origin of his people? She ran her fingers softly across his brow, following the curve of his face, and cradled his jaw with her hand.

They'd connected somehow, though she wasn't sure on what level. She would stay with him until he was well and then, as promised, he would take her to the fort. There was no reason for her to believe otherwise.

The hours stretched out in endless succession, his delirium causing him to jerk in his sleep. On brief occasions he would wake long enough to receive two or three drops of tea, before slipping back into sleep.

Many times in the hours that followed, Sarah pondered whether to try to find his people, but she remembered him saying they were leaving for the mountains. Which brought up another puzzling question. *Why?* What possible force was strong enough to cause an entire group of people to willingly leave the land of their forefathers?

She knew in brief, the problems that some of the Cherokee had with the white settlers, though only the side of the government was greatly publicized. More often than not, the Cherokee people were referred to as less than human. Sarah sighed, her heart saddened by the possible truth of the description given the savagery of what she'd seen, yet it was difficult to think of White Eagle in the same capacity.

She made the decision after much internal debate to stay with him and take the chance his sumac tea remedy would provide adequate healing. There was little doubt in her mind that her presence was his only chance at this point, and certainly his presence was paramount to her and Isabella's survival.

CHAPTER EIGHT

Brewing Storm

The visions in White Eagle's dreams swirled together like grains of sand in a desert storm. The sky turned black, streaked red and churning with the eddy of a mystic pool. On a ridge, he stood; his silhouette etched against the sky, below stretched a valley covered in winter's snow. Dotting the land for miles was a trail of humanity—his people, thousands upon thousands—snaked toward the horizon as far as the eye could see, yet he was unable to move, to reach out, or follow them.

Gazing at his feet, he discovered thick iron shackles that stayed him to the spot where he stood. With all his might he struggled to walk, to even lift his foot, yet the despairing weight made it impossible. A fierce wind blew frigid bursts of air around him, while fingers of icy particles froze his exposed skin, making it numb.

Far below, the cries of his people—Cherokee women and children—mixed with the despondent moan of the wind. He dropped to his knees, praying to the Great Spirit to help his people in their distress, but only the wind howling with the roar of a great rapid answered.

He could not save them.

White Eagle's body jerked as he awoke suddenly from the dream. Darkness enveloped everything, save the small flame casting its grotesque shadows against the cave walls. Through the rippling haze of heat rising from the fire, he saw her. The woman called Sarah; her chin dropped to her chest, resting peacefully, her body propped against the cave's wall.

He had to find a way to get her and the child to the camp. If Tsula and his people found her alive, they would no doubt use them in some form for retaliation or bargaining. Though he abhorred the unjust attacks on the peaceful clans, to retaliate with pain for pain was not the answer. To use an innocent to gain your advantage, on either side, was against his own principles. He could not let this happen.

White Eagle glanced wearily at the infant child sleeping near her on the pallet. There was no explanation for the ties he had toward this woman and her child. The sooner he had them safe within the walls of the fort, the sooner he could join his people, far from the darkness soon to overshadow the Cherokee.

"Have you found him?" Tsula stirred the ashes of the fire pit, and watched the flames licking at the small rabbit carcass.

The scout had searched the mountains and spied on several of the white settler's camps looking for the man his leader bid him to find. "It is though the Great Spirit has taken him, Tsula."

Tsula frowned as he stared into the fire. He'd only wanted to incapacitate White Eagle. Not kill him. Though the thought sickened him, he could not cast aside the nagging fear that something worse had happened. That he'd managed to escape and had this woman and her child with him. Tsula squinted through the smoke. What need would he have with a white woman and her child? "You found nothing? Not a body, nor that of a woman with a child?"

The loyal Indian shook his head no.

"Did you speak to his sister, Running Doe? Has she seen him?"

The warrior nodded as he stood on the other side of the fire, eyeing the roasting meat hungrily. "She has not seen him. She asked of you." The man licked his lips, and glanced at Tsula.

With his focus trained on the fire, Tsula weighed carefully his words. "There is more to be done now. My vision does not include taking a wife and having children. It is my duty to see that there is a Cherokee nation left from which our people shall endure." He tore off a piece of the charred meat and held it between his fingers.

"You are wise in this, Tsula. White Eagle does not understand what needs to be done. We," he motioned to the few tribesmen scattered on the ground, some sleeping, others sharpening their arrows, "are the ones who will preserve our lineage."

Tsula thought about his friend. Once he and White Eagle had been inseparable—blood brothers—so close they knew every crevice of the mountains and valleys. All the best places to hide when one didn't want to be found. They would pride themselves in competing to see who could find the best hideout.

Tsula stared into the orange flames, leaping and crackling as fat splattered its heat. Suddenly he knew where White Eagle was.

"You must surely be hungry after your searching. Here, eat." Tsula glanced quickly at the anxious warrior, and then cast his gaze to the stars. He had not wanted it to come to this, but there was the traditional law of balance among his people to think about. Had so many quickly forgotten the events of years past that left the bloody carnage of his people in the lower Cherokee villages?

This recent sacrifice of white settler's satiated the wrong done then, and restored the harmony of the land. Why couldn't White Eagle understand this? Even now, news spread that the great chief of the White people had signed a private treaty to force the Cherokee from this land, despite the futile efforts of a handful of noble white men named Clay, Webster, and Worcester. This treaty, though only signed by a few hundred Cherokee did not reflect the feelings of the entire Cherokee Nation.

Once, during a Red Clay council, Tsula had heard Chief John Ross speak out against the treaty. Already the white man had taken land, possessions, and livestock from some tribes, yet they wanted more. He knew his destiny and he knew he would not be moved from the land of his people, no matter what the cost.

White Eagle struggled to sit up, but a wave of dizziness besieged him. He slumped back to the floor, his body weak from lying on the hard floor and the longevity of his fever.

A bitter, coppery taste lingered on his tongue and he remembered the sumac potion, but how she got it down him was a hazy blur—at best—in his memory.

Vague snippets of his memory floated in his mind, ghostly apparitions, yet strong in his spirit remained the sweet scent of her skin. This woman, who could have made the choice to abandon him, to leave him to die, for what loyalty did she bear him? A part of him harbored great satisfaction that she had stayed, while another reasoned her choice was more for the sake of the child's survival.

Another wave of nausea swept over him and he swallowed the bile rising in his throat. Through fatigue, he focused on the ceiling, commanding his body to right itself, calling on the Great Spirit to heal him. He was surprised to see the small patch of blue through the hole in the cave ceiling. As he waited for his stomach to cease its churning, he watched the clouds through blurred vision, and his mind drifted back to the last conversation he had with his sister.

"Tsula would not do this thing which you blame him of." Running Doe shook her head no as she stared at him in disbelief.

White Eagle methodically continued his task of gathering food, he was anxious to return to the woman and her child and even more so not to risk being caught by Tsula. It would not benefit him to tell his sister that the very wound that now disabled came at the hands of her intended. She would likely become angry and perhaps not listen to the greater, more important matters he needed to discuss with her.

"You are hurt. Let me see." She approached, reaching out to touch his bandage, a frown etching her soft brown face.

He eased from her touch and placed his free hand on her arm. There was much to say and little time to explain. White Eagle gazed at her intently as he spoke, "You must listen. The door has opened to the fury that is to follow. Neither you, nor I, wish this on our people, but neither do we have the power to stop the evil that fans the greed of men."

The expression in her eyes signaled her undivided attention.

"Once we talked of taking our clan to the mountains. The time has come. You must prepare tonight and leave before daylight." His gaze narrowed on hers, hoping she would see the grave urgency in his words.

She returned his gaze in silence and even as she glanced away, he knew she understood. She had felt the same tremors in the balance of her spirit. He had sensed as much.

"Soon the rivers will run red with the blood of many. Our future rests in our hands. We must protect it. We must hide until the evil has passed. Then we will be a free people once more."

"Will we come back, when the time is right?" Her worried gaze searched his.

"I cannot say. My dreams only speak of dangers and the death of many." He could offer no more.

Her gaze locked into his. "These are your visions?"

Wishing with all that was in him, that he could shelter her from the inevitable, he touched her face. All of their life, she had cared for him, educated him, been his best friend, and confidant and now he could only ask her to leave all she'd ever known to be true and good with little explanation.

"It is to be. I cannot change what is to come."

Apprehension etched her gentle features. "Where will you go? Why are you not traveling with us?"

"I am going to the cave near the Eagle's nest." He

wanted to tell her about the woman and child he held in hiding, but concern for her safety interceded. The less his sister knew this time, the better for her and his people.

"And why are you taking food for more than a few days?" Her voice piqued with concern.

He turned away from her questioning gaze and felt it boring into his back. "There is a woman." White Eagle did not need to turn around to know the look on his sister's face. "She survived the attack."

"The massacre, one you say Tsula led these tribesmen to, yes?"

His shoulder ached, as did his head. He needed to leave soon while he had the strength to get back to the cave. "I cannot speak to you now of this. You must do as I say. I will join you in a few days."

White Eagle parted the blanket guarding the hut's entrance. His sister followed doggedly on his heel. He tossed the deerskin pouch over the back of the appaloosa and shifted its contents. He was nervous to leave such grave responsibility at the feet of his sister. The council would be difficult to convince, but he had confidence in her powers of persuasion. He'd lived with it all of his life. Besides once the settlers discovered the news of the attack, the terror upon the tribes would serve as confirmation of his unusual request.

He grabbed the gray mane of his horse and pulled himself astride its back, glancing down at his sister's hand on his knee.

"She is worth the trouble of sacrifice, my brother?" Running Doe handed the reins up to him, narrowing her curious gaze.

Faced with the truth, White Eagle realized, as did his

sister, the peril he brought to their lives—the woman's, the child's, and his. If his plan succeeded, the woman and child would be safe and he would go back to the ways of his people. Tsula and his men would be on their own to deal with the impending danger.

"She is innocent," he replied, pulling his reins to the side, maneuvering to leave. "I will get her to the white man's fort and then join you in the mountains."

"Is she wounded as well?" Running Doe grabbed his leg as he tried to leave.

"I have not determined if that is so, but this much is certain. What she has seen this day gives her little reason to trust the Cherokee."

"Yet, you are sure she waits even now for your return." Her brow quirked in a way a woman's does when she knows the truth of a matter.

"She is wise in knowing that to get lost in the forest would only bring her harm. She wishes to be taken on to her destination."

"Why do you wait?"

He frowned, growing more impatient with his chattering sister. "I do not understand your question."

"Why have you not taken her straight to the camp? Why do you insist on hiding her as a prisoner in a cave?"

She'd managed to corner him again. The woman was crafty.

He tamped down his frustration, "I could not risk riding into the white man's camp with a woman and her—" he stopped, unwilling to go further. "You must trust what I do—and she *is not* my prisoner."

Running Doe dropped her hold on his leg. "I trust your word, my brother. It is your heart which concerns me."

His sister's concern mirrored his own.

CHAPTER NINE

The Many Faces of Truth

Startled abruptly from her dozing, Sarah listened intently. Someone was coming up through the cave entrance. She scrambled to her feet and assessed quickly that White Eagle still slept where she'd left him. Isabella lay curled asleep on her pallet blissfully unaware of any danger.

Sarah glanced toward the hole in the ceiling where she could see the remnants of stars, in the early dawn sky. She reached down, searching the floor with her hand as she fixed her gaze on the entrance.

Finding a rock, the size that fit her hand, she curled her fingers around it and straightened, prepared for a physical encounter. She raised the stone above her head.

"White Eagle?"

The soft voice of a woman surprised Sarah. She blinked as she bent down, dropping the stone, curious about the unexpected visitor.

A beautiful woman appeared from the cave entrance, capturing Sarah's surprised gaze. Her hair hung loose, straight, and as jet-black as White Eagle's. Her eyes too, were shaped much the same and color as his.

She smiled and tipped her head slightly.

Her face appeared friendly and for an instant she realized how much she missed Emily.

"So, you are the one my brother is protecting."

Protecting? The woman's command of English was remarkable and at closer study of her features Sarah discovered that she possessed the same intense and direct gaze as her brother.

"*You* are White Eagle's sister?" Sarah had many questions forming in her mind, but she held them at bay not wanting to frighten the woman.

"Yes, my name is Running Doe."

"I don't understand this need for protection? I understand yes, from the wild, but do you mean from the Indi—" She paused reworking her own prejudices into her words. "From those men who attacked us?"

Sarah wanted to learn more of what this woman appeared to know. Even more curious was why had she come to the cave?

"Us?" The woman glanced around the cave, her gaze settling on her brother. Oblivious now to Sarah, she brushed past and knelt beside White Eagle. She glanced at the broken gourd and picked it up, sniffing its cold contents. "You have given him this?" She tipped the disintegrated remains of the bowl. "How long ago?"

Fear crept into her heart and Sarah hoped suddenly she'd followed the proper instructions. She made a rapid assessment of his brief commands, and then blurted out, "He told me to first crush the mountain sumac." She jabbed her index finger to her palm as she replayed his words in her head. Sarah motioned with her hands in frantic gestures trying to use them to emphasize her thoughts. It was a habit she knew that Miss Emma, on more than one occasion, tried to cure her of. Emily explained with confidence that it was simply the storyteller in her.

"He then said to boil the leaves into a tea." Her mind whirled. Had she followed the instructions correctly? She turned a frightened gaze to the man who had not moved since last night. Oh Lord! Perhaps she'd killed him!

"You have done just as you should. The tea will help his fever. My brother owes you his life. Our people believe there is a balance to all things." She glanced up, giving Sarah a smile. "You have cared for him, now he must care for you."

Relief washed over her as the thought of his obligation sunk in. *What exactly did she mean by 'care of you?'*

"He has already done so much…I mean, did." Sarah glanced at White Eagle. A fine sheen of perspiration covered him. Fever continued to rack his body and she searched her mind, grappling with what more she could do to ease his suffering.

She turned her gaze to the woman. "He saved us from those," she paused, not wanting to refer to them as savages, though it is the term their behavior deserved. "He's already risked his life." She turned to his sister. "I don't know why he chose save us."

Running Doe brushed her palm across White Eagle's forehead. "Perhaps you are needed for some greater good."

The thought left Sarah more than a little concerned. She opened her mouth, ready to speak, but Running Doe interrupted.

"He will need much rest and more sumac tea to drive the fever from him." She stood and turned to leave. "Come."

Confused, Sarah followed her movement, and then stared back at White Eagle. *Surely she did not intend to leave him here?* "Wait. What shall we do? Is there a way to take him with us? What abou—" Her hands motioned to

White Eagle.

Her compassionate gaze met Sarah's, and then dropped to where her brother lay.

The woman's quiet gasp was enough for Sarah to know she'd seen Isabella.

"It is good of you to think of my brother's well-being. He will follow when he is rested. It is best we not move him. Here, he is safe." Running Doe glanced at Sarah. "He would wish for you to come with us. You and the child."

Sarah's eyes widened in disbelief. "You can't just expect to leave him here—alone? What about wild animals? What if he should need something? He has no strength." She caught the studious gaze of the capable young woman and felt her cheeks warm.

The words burst from her mouth before she gave herself the chance to think. "I will stay with him until he is well."

The lone cry of a hawk in the distance broke the momentary silence.

"And what of the child?" The woman bent down, scooping the sleeping infant into her arms. "Her skin is pale, when did she eat last?"

Sarah swallowed; the hard lump of guilt mixed with fear as she squared her shoulders and gazed directly into the woman's soft brown eyes. "I am not her mother." It felt good to tell someone, for the truth to be out. "Her mother is dead, as well as her father, I presume." Tears welled in Sarah's eyes as she struggled past the horrid memory. *Was it only yesterday? Two days?*

"What has she eaten?" Running Doe inspected Isabella, closely examining her. The child no longer cried, and only stared at the woman holding her.

The guilt became unbearable, "Sugar water I'm afraid. It's all I had, I didn't know what else to do, I—" Her words muffled as she lowered her face into her hands and sobbed.

A gentle touch startled her and she glanced up, her gaze locking into that of the young Cherokee woman. Compassion and warmth stared back at her.

"I will take her with me. There are women, new mothers, with much milk to share. We will care for her as you have cared for my brother. When he is well, he will bring you to get the child."

She smiled at the baby in her arms. "What is her name?"

Sarah blinked, intrigued why the child had not uttered one sound while in Running Doe's arms. "Um, it's Isabella—" She realized she did not remember the child's last name. A sob stuck in her throat. "I'm not so certain… what if he…doesn't get well?" Sarah knew in her heart that Isabella's best chance of survival was to go with Running Doe. She would be safe with White Eagle's people.

"My brother has a strong body and has strength here—" She pointed to her head and then to her heart. "And here." She offered a knowing smile like that of a sister who knew her brother all too well. "It is *you* who will need the strength of the Great Spirit to give you wisdom and White Eagle will need your wisdom to give him strength."

Running Doe shifted Isabella over her shoulder. "We are going into the mountains. There we will be safe." She explained nothing further.

Sarah wanted to ask her more, but she sensed time was of the essence.

Running Doe knelt beside her brother. "It is the two

of you who must heed caution. It is a two-day ride from here. We must be on our way."

"Is it those who attacked the settlers that we hide from?" Sarah needed to know who or what she was up against.

Running Doe nodded. "For now, you hide from both Cherokee and white man."

She placed a gentle hand on Sarah's arm searching her face. "There is much unrest in our land at this time. Do you understand?"

Sarah nodded, though in truth her concern was narrowed down to the lives of those around her. She wondered if her father was well, or if he too, was out looking for her? The sooner she got to the camp, the better for all of them.

Running Doe gently kissed White Eagle's rugged cheek, and then stood cradling Isabella as if she were her own. "You will join us soon. I will leave you blankets, cloth for more bandages, and food for two days' travel."

"You are kind to do this." Sarah wrung her hands, a part of her yet unsure about letting Isabella from her sight.

By the time Running Doe returned with their supplies, she had Isabella snuggled into a blanket tied across her body.

The Cherokee woman sensed her concern. "You needn't worry. I have helped care for many of our clan's children." She glanced at Isabella. "One day I hope to have many of my own, should the Great Spirit grant me that gift."

Sarah reached into the blanket touching Isabella's tiny fist once more and reassurance washed over her. "I know you will take care of her. Thank you."

Running Doe glanced back at her brother. "It is I who should thank you."

Several miniscule doses of sumac tea later, Sarah sat huddled by the fire, her pencil recording furiously the events of the past few hours. She wrote of meeting Running Doe and of how the Indian woman had treated Isabella as one of her own, taking her to the mountains to be properly cared for. And she wrote of the things White Eagle had spoken of in the delirium of his fever. In broken English, sometimes giving way to his native tongue, he spoke of grave, ghastly images, of thousands dying and the screams of the wind in the dark sky. His moans, laced with pain and sorrow, reminded her of a wounded animal.

Sarah shivered as she reread her words, and then sat for a time simply watching the rise and fall of White Eagle's chest as he slept. He'd lapsed into a quieter slumber over the past few hours, giving her more time to ponder the things he'd said. She made a note to ask White Eagle a few questions when he was better able to handle them. Sighing, she stirred again at the fire to keep it burning bright. If she could manage to survive the next few days, she would surely have much to write to Emily about.

White Eagle's tumultuous nightmares faded into a dreamless sleep—deep and void of the disturbing images that had previously taunted his mind over the past few hours. His body ached from sheer fatigue and he attempted to shift from his back to sit up. Slumping down, he realized his body lacked the strength to hold itself upright.

Instead he turned his head and tried with great effort to open his eyes.

"You should not try to move so fast. You have been ill and no doubt you are weak with hunger. I am making you some more tea. Perhaps you are ready to eat something?"

Her voice smoothed over him with the coolness of a waterfall on a hot day. He reached up; fingering the tepid cloth spread over his forehead and pulled it over his face. Her sweet scent permeated every fiber as it refreshed his skin.

There was no way of knowing for sure how long he'd slept, but his stomach growled in protest for food.

"Indeed, it appears you are hungry. That, I would think, is a good sign."

White Eagle forced open his eyelids, squinting against the firelight, its shadows dancing on the cave walls. He tried to gage the time, tried to remember anything, but his thoughts scattered as he came into focus.

She sat near the fire, stirring the contents of a bowl he recognized as one of his sister's. Words stayed lodged in his brain, unable to find their way through his mouth. His throat was thick as honeycomb.

"Drink this, your sister brought it." The woman who called herself Sarah tucked her arm beneath his neck and pulled him up until he rested against her like a child. Holding the small clay vessel near his lips, she prompted him to drink.

He jerked from the foreign taste and coughed, wincing as he tried to support himself on his wounded arm.

"You are as stubborn as your sister indicates, Mr. White Eagle."

Her reprimanding tone caused him to offer her a stern

glance only to be surprised when she smiled in return.

Frowning, White Eagle averted his gaze to the drink still held in her hand. His face lingered too closely to where he had yet to see her feed the child. The thought of it both disturbed and confused him. He glanced around the cave realizing the child was not on her pallet.

"The child?" His voice was heavy, sounding angrier than he'd intended. The stark look of panic was clear on her face as she tried to lay him back to the floor and scoot away from him.

He grabbed for her arm, his palm instead encasing one soft breast. Shocked as much as she was, he froze.

Sarah's eyes widened in fright and her body went rigid.

He dropped his hand immediately, contrite for his mistake. "I am sorry," he mumbled, a part of him surprised that he should be saddened at her fearful response.

"Uh…" She glanced away obviously flustered. "Your sister, Running Doe took Isabella to the mountains until you are well enough to take me to her."

"When was she here?" His eyes stung from being closed for so long.

"Earlier this morning." She cleared her throat and edged away from him.

"Why did she take the child?" White Eagle shifted laboriously until his back could rest against the wall.

He glanced at his shoulder and could see that at some point someone had changed his bandages. Though it was still sore, the pain was not as sharp. He was also aware she'd not answered his other question.

He reached for the cup in her hand, his body in desperate need of the nourishment she offered.

She held it out to him as frightened as a trapped animal.

"I will not harm you." He sipped the drink, eyeing her over the rim. Brushing two fingers over his mouth, he studied her reaction. Her face was easy to read.

The timid woman he'd accidentally embraced straightened and moved so that the small campfire was between them. "I didn't think you would, Mr. Eagle."

"It is White Eagle. 'Mr.' is a white man's term."

"Which is used to show respect to the person it is directed toward."

Were all white women as determined as this one?

"Then you will call me, Mr. White Eagle."

Her gaze riveted to his and for a moment he met a challenge so strong that a shiver ran up his spine.

"What of the child?" A quick detour of his thoughts cut off the look of challenge before what crossed his mind would surely have made him seem an untamed savage. In truth, since he'd awoken to her face at the site of the ambush, her strength and simple beauty intrigued him. The fact that she remained to care for him jangled his normal complacency regarding women. Though not opposed entirely to the idea, he was in no hurry to settle down, much less have a family. Why he should think of that at a time like this confused him all the more.

"I felt she was safer with your people." Sarah focused on re-fluffing the straw of her pallet.

"Safe? You believe this even after all you have seen?" He tipped his head, his eyes searching her face looking for a sign that she was hiding something more.

She met his gaze, and her green eyes shone in the flickering light. The purity of her innocence sparked dangerous emotions within him.

"She said there were mothers who could," she swallowed, visibly nervous, "feed her properly."

The undertone in her voice caused an unwelcome suspicion that snaked into his thoughts and they warred with his neat image of the innocence of her.

"It must be difficult to apart from her." He would not let his mind wander into directions that would lead to certain trouble. He needed fresh air and he had the desire to wash his body of the fevered state that had imprisoned him for two days.

Thanks to the Great Spirit and the unselfish care of Sarah.

He struggled to stand, reaching out to brace the wall rather than take the hand she offered him. "I am going to the river."

"Should you go alone?"

As much as a part of him wanted to allow the image of her skin glowing in the light of the harvest moon, he reminded himself she was another man's wife and he was an honorable man. He had an inexplicable desire to show her that the Cherokee people were not like those she'd met. Most were gentle, educated, and honorable in many ways.

Still it was hard to refocus his thoughts, given her gentle tone of concern. He had to remind himself that she was merely concerned for his health.

He must push these carnal thoughts aside and not let himself be captivated by his mere curiosity of this woman.

"Did Running Doe leave us food?" He noted his heart quickened as he stared at her and he reprimanded himself, turning his gaze quickly from hers.

"I will prepare something warm for you. You need nourishment and rest."

His gaze returned briefly to hers, stopping long enough to see her cheeks color a pale pink. While it was not his desire to have her serve him in any way that implied familiarity, he determined the task would at least keep her busy. That way he would have time to assess the war going on between his head and his loins.

"Good." From now on, he would keep their conversations brief. The less they knew of one another's lives, the easier it would be to stay in close proximity to each other. He was after all an average man, and he could not deny her beauty. To think of that combined with her compassion and gentle concern was more than White Eagle wanted to deal with.

He left quickly, avoiding further eye contact and looked forward to the freezing river water from the mountains, knowing they could heal a man of many things.

CHAPTER TEN

Tender Beginning

Silence was their companion as they nibbled on flat-bread and salt=dried deer meat. Outwardly, his body was cleansed of the fever due to his bout of illness, but a fever of greater concern smoldered inside and no icy river would satisfy it.

This woman called Sarah was shy, innocent in so many ways, yet strong, almost to the point of defiant. Pride, he concluded, was apparently not exclusive to Cherokee women. Perhaps it was the odd color of her eyes he found so fascinating.

He smiled softly as he kept his gaze on the floor. Perhaps it was her passion for proper etiquette, like when she insisted on calling him, *Mr.* White Eagle. Whatever it was, conscious or implied; she stirred something far more curious in him than any woman he'd known before. She had a quick wit and an inquisitive mind and if once she'd truly been afraid since they'd been together, she'd kept it carefully concealed.

The list of her likeable attributes gave him pause, signaling him to change the direction of his thoughts. As surely as there were many pleasing qualities in this woman, there were as many—if not more—as unlikable should he take a moment to study them.

Instead, he chose to venture into conversation. "Surely, you miss your Isabella." His difficulty with the pronunciation of the child's name reminded him with razor precision of the vast cultural differences between them. Any foolish, young boy fantasy he had entertained dissipated in a puff of smoke.

"What kind of mother would I be if I did not, Mr. White Eagle?" She peeled off a strip of meat, inspecting it carefully before placing it between her teeth.

He swallowed hard as he watched her nibble daintily at the food. She had no idea how powerfully her simple gesture affected him, and in truth, he was surprised himself. He shifted, clearing his throat hoping to do the same with the images in his mind.

"Do you have children?" She licked the end of her thumb, and ran her tongue over her bottom lip.

He watched mesmerized, forgetting completely what she'd asked.

"Is that a forbidden subject?"

He met her thoughtful gaze and blinked. "No."

She tipped her head and continued to hold his gaze. "Well?"

He closed his eyes, frowning as he tried to remember what it was she had asked.

"I asked if you had children."

He nodded; not at all sure he cared for the way this woman was able to bewitch him with her manner, her soft voice, those captivating eyes. "Yes, I remember," he lied, and then reprimanded himself mentally for demeaning his character in such a way. "I have not yet taken a wife"

She blushed openly, dropping her gaze to her lap.

Part of him sensed a small triumph in that. Perhaps she should be shown that she was not the only curious one between them.

"And what of your husband?" The reality of another man in her life hit him with the force of a branch between the eyes. There'd been someone who woke each morning to her smile, someone who'd heard her sighs in the middle of the night.

White Eagle suddenly lost his appetite. His stomach churned and he grimaced at the thought of one more bite of food. It was the food and nothing more. He'd almost convinced himself "I must go to the river." He stood purposely avoiding her startled gaze.

"Again? Are you sure you have the strength?"

If there was one thing White Eagle was completely sure of, it was his strength, yet not for the same reasons. "Finish your food," he commanded roughly, pointing to her meat.

"Thank you, sir; I had every intention of doing so."

He closed his eyes at her blatant mocking tone; frustrated that it should arouse him

"What is the report, Captain?" He shuffled the papers, tapping them to the small worn desk he'd borrowed from the mess hall. He'd been immersed in checking the receipts for last month's gold find and while he was pleased with the results, he knew, given more time and territory, he could easily double, maybe triple those numbers.

Those redskins who'd cooperated fully with his business were compensated handsomely with food, clothing, and livestock for their loyalty.

"Report says twenty-three dead, sir. Mostly men." The messenger hesitated causing the man to look up from his work. He could tell his steady gaze made the green horn soldier a tad nervous. It was nice to know his abilities still worked for him.

"No women?"

"Only one, sir. There is a report of a woman and a child missing." The soldier kept his gaze pinpointed to the wall, his shoulders stiff at attention.

The man sighed. "When are the remains slated to arrive?"

"Sir, sometime around daybreak, sir"

"You can dispense with calling me sir. I'm not your commanding officer." *Though he could probably handle it as well as some of the nation's finest.*

"Uh, yes si—" The soldier glanced at him, and then quickly looked away.

"Never mind. Just notify me when they arrive." He waved a hand in dismissal.

Perhaps tonight it was not wise to ride with his men. If this band of Cherokee were indicative of the climate among those in the territory, any major retaliation for this massacre could inflate into a full scale war. A war, which at present the American government was unprepared to wage. A well-placed letter to the governor would give him the legislative support he needed. He made a note to speak to the officer in charge of the special regiment of volunteer soldiers assigned to this secondary mission of the white settler's progress. In the meantime, what the government didn't know wouldn't hurt them. He and his men would find a way to deal with the matter of stubborn Indians in a show that would hopefully intimidate enough of them to achieve their objective.

It was clear that Congress intended to continue to drag its feet with what needed to be done. Though his committee had sent repeated findings of Indians who showed stubborn, willful attitudes toward the generous relocation efforts.

With their so-called alphabet and mission schools, not to mention the National Indian council of government, there were simply too many and they were becoming too knowledgeable for their own good.

And now this? What more proof did they need?

If the new president could not persuade the do-gooders in Washington, then they would handle the situation themselves. It would have been a hell of a lot easier if they'd left the land peaceably.

With a great sigh he pulled the stubby cork from the neck of a small whiskey decanter, swirling what was left in the bottom. He inhaled deeply its contents and in his mind toasted better days, with plenty of this and more for those willing to envision it and to those who knew that with progress there was also sacrifice.

He tipped the bottle back, letting the amber liquid trickle down his throat. Clenching his teeth to the searing heat of its potency, he stared at the framed picture on his desk.

∞

Sarah stared into the fire, watching the yellow and blue flames dance merrily over the twigs. The snap and crackle of pine needles lulled her into a sense of security and warmth, something she noted she'd experienced lately, especially in the presence of White Eagle.

He had been truthful with her. Would it not be wise to be the same with him? Should she tell him about Isabella? Certainly at some point, he was going to discover the truth. For the sake of honesty—after all, she did owe him her life—she decided to tell him the truth.

Sarah turned when she heard his footsteps, her gaze catching his expression as he came through the entrance. The look was unspecific, but he almost appeared angry. Fear struck her belly as she watched him return to where he'd been seated. How would he take this news? Would he see it as an open invitation to her virginity? Chills skimmed over her arms, unsure of her reaction to that possibility. Part of her questioned the wisdom of the truth, while another part of her wanted him to know she was not committed to anyone—as absurd a notion as that was.

White Eagle warmed his hands over the fire, ignoring her presence. His hair, plastered down his back from the lake, gave greater definition to his shoulders. He shifted, trying to work out the kinks in the muscles of his back using his good shoulder.

Mesmerized, Sarah did her best to stay focused on telling him the truth. "I have a confession to make." She averted her gaze to the small childlike etchings on the cave wall. A silence, long and warm stretched out between them.

He yawned, extending his good arm overhead, at the very least unaware, or simply unconcerned with her open attempt at absolution.

The apathy in return was unexpected and more of a blow to her unprepared self-esteem. Not to mention his simple gesture pulled her attention to the perfection of his chiseled torso, heating up her thoughts with images that she, as a well-bred, educated woman, should *not* be entertaining.

He didn't prod her for a confession, in fact did not

acknowledge that having a conversation with her on any level was a matter of priority. Something in the revelation bothered Sarah. She wasn't sure what it was she wanted from him. Perhaps it was best left alone, not to be over-analyzed. Still, to reveal to him the truth of Isabella's mother, she would have nothing to defend herself with. Nothing but simple morals would stop that which might naturally occur when two adults found themselves alone and attracted to one another, provided both adults were consenting.

She covered her mouth with the hand, appalled such an idea would foster in her head. Then again, perhaps she was concerned she wouldn't have to deal with the con-senting part?

"Are you ill?" His low-timbered voice caused a jittery sensation in her stomach and areas where proper ladies didn't think of—generally. She wasn't a prude. Emily had made sure she knew about what happens between a man and a woman when they married. She just never men-tioned that one might entertain those thoughts prior to marriage.

She shook her head vigorously—no.

"You miss the child?"

"Yes, of course," she squeaked out, her throat con-stricting from nerves.

"And your husband as well?"

Sarah knew now they had reached the point she'd hoped to avoid, but with all that had happened, she was tired of pretending. If there was ever going to be total un-derstanding between the Cherokee and the white settler's, shouldn't it begin with the simple ability to be truthful and open in their communication?

"No…I mean, yes," she stuttered searching for the easiest way to explain. Sarah covered her eyes with her hand, yet sensed his studious gaze. Parting her fingers, she confirmed her suspicions as his dark eyes captured her heart at once. She knew it was wrong to keep him thinking she had a family, yet she was concerned that the raw attraction churning inside her was also dangerously wrong.

"Was your husband killed in the attack?" The gentle tone in his voice quelled her nerves-some.

"No." She clasped her hands together firmly in her lap and held his gaze. "What I am attempting to say, Mr. White Eagle…is that I have no husband." She waited for his reaction.

The brow over his right eye rose briefly as he turned his gaze to the fire, continuing to warm his hands.

Sarah stumbled on, freed at last from the lies she'd been harboring inside her after all the good he'd shown them. "I didn't mean to lie, exactly. I was afraid of what you might do to me or Isabella." The weight of her burden shifted from her shoulders, and she sensed relief, though confused about his reaction. Perhaps it simply did not matter to him?

"Because you thought you'd have the same fate as the others?" He returned a slow and steady gaze to hers.

To deny the truth would be wrong. She could only shrug and hope he would understand.

"We are not all savages, Sarah." He picked up a stick and stirred the flaming embers.

She stared at the fire with him in silence, watching tiny sparks explode into a feathery display of light, floating down into the gray ash.

"We are a gentle people—peaceful and wise. We have

great regard and respect for all living things."

"I never questioned—" she interjected hoping to find the degree of connection she'd felt to him moments before.

"We are also an intelligent people, with thoughts and emotions not so unlike yours." He smiled. "Who is she? The child?"

"Isabella is the daughter of a woman who was riding in the back of the wagon you pulled me from." Sarah wrung her hands in her lap, twisting a portion of her skirt between her fingers. "She handed her to me just before—" she gulped for air to quell the queasiness in her stomach, —"before the wagon slipped backward over the ridge. I heard a scream. She must have fallen from the back and the wagon landed on top of her." Caught in the horrific memory, Sarah stared blankly at the fire. "That's where I found her—later—when I went to get Isabella's bag." She covered her mouth; sure she was going to be sick.

"You are a brave woman, Sarah."

She shook her head. Too many emotions erupted in her heart and she finally wept for the release of them.

"My father once told me that it takes a strong man to cry. I trust the wisdom holds true for a woman as well."

"I feel so ashamed. Why should I live, and Isabella's mother die? How is it that *I am here* and not Laura?" Tears streaked her cheeks and she knew her eyes were puffy and red as they always were when she cried.

"No one can question the gods, Sarah." His gaze captured hers and for the first time she saw him not as an imposing stranger, but as someone she respected and admired—a friend who understood pain.

"I didn't want to be untruthful with you; it's just that I

didn't know if I could—"

"Trust me?" His eyes searched hers.

"I suppose that's it then, isn't it?" she warbled her smile weak and tears clogging her throat.

He nodded as he stood and walked to her side. Kneeling beside her, he spoke quietly, "Do you trust me now?"

Her throat tightened from fear—or perhaps desire—she could not tell. The heat inside the cave made her light-headed as she held his gaze.

His fingers, calloused but gentle, brushed across her cheeks, gently wiping away the tracks of her tears. "I am about to return my gratitude."

Mesmerized, she watched his face as it drew close until her mind surrendered to the inevitable.

His mouth tentatively touched hers and Sarah ducked from the sensation.

"Does this not please you?" His breath whispered soft against her forehead.

Closing her eyes, she gave little thought to the moral dilemma—what her father would do if he found out, or how badly her heart would break when the time would come that she must leave him. For now, pleasing him and being pleased by him were foremost in her mind and in her heart.

"I don't know, I'm afraid." Honest words. It felt right to finally be honest, but if she were truly, shouldn't he also know how he affected her? "It does please me. God help me it does. I want you to kiss me again."

He grinned, instantly melting away her concern. "An odd prayer."

She frowned, but her questions were lost as his mouth sought hers. Sarah succumbed to the strange, yet pleasing sensation of a man's lips touching hers. Only in her dreams had one ever actually accomplished the task. Yet in her dreams that man was gentle and passionate with dark eyes who smelled of the earth and sun.

White Eagle pulled her to her knees, grasping her waist with his good arm. Carefully, he touched her face, offering gentle kisses to her brows, her eyelids, traveling with excruciating slowness toward her mouth.

Closing her eyes, she allowed his tender exploration, her heart pounding with anticipation. A muffled cry emitted from her throat when at last he kissed her again, more soundly than the first, seeking her surrender with the urgent movement of his mouth over hers.

Odd sensations began to assault her and regardless of her inexperience, Sarah could not deny the warmth beginning to liquefy her bones. With a startled gasp, she grabbed his shoulders to keep from tumbling back.

White Eagle pulled away with a painful grimace on his face.

Surprised at his sudden retreat, then flustered she came to the realization of her *faux pas*. "I'm sorry. I'm so sorry." She moved next to him, gently turning his shoulder toward the light to inspect for any new damage. Timid in her investigation she tenderly kissed the exposed skin of his shoulder.

"Sarah." His breath hitched as he swallowed. He took her hand and held it to his chest. "You have not been with a man."

The heat rushed into her face so quickly she had no time to hide it. She turned, wanting to disappear, embarrassed that her naiveté' was so apparent.

"I thought not." His finger lifted her chin to his gaze.

Sarah wanted to be with him more than anything, but the compassionate look in his steady gaze made her realize that it would not happen tonight—perhaps not ever—not with him. An excruciating stab of loss penetrated her heart.

"You do not find me attractive." She tried not to sound as though she was a pouting ninny. She glanced at her torn blouse and the smudges of ash on her forearms, sure that her face must look the same.

With a sudden swift movement of his hand over hers, he pressed her palm, unashamed, against his manhood. "Does it appear that I do not find you attractive, Sarah?"

Her eyes widened in astonishment more than the blunt action of truth. She glanced, uncertain, to where their hands lay together then followed his movement as he brought her palm to his cheek.

Gently he kissed the inside of her wrist, her concerns washed away in the bliss of tingles racing down her arm.

"What I feel for you is not like what I have felt for women before you."

She fought hard to understand the confusing emotions skating through her. How could she have such passionate feelings for someone so different from herself?

"But it is unwise to satisfy these urges."

The gentle caress of his gaze moved her hand to his mouth, closing the distance between them. Unwise or not, she was infatuated with this strange man she'd only known a few hours, yet sensed she'd known in her heart, a lifetime. "You are exquisitely beautiful. Your body, your heart, your mind." She could barely breathe the admission as she traced her finger over the fullness of his lower lip. To say these words to a man had never occurred to her before, but the words came with sincerity and she did not regret them.

White Eagle closed his eyes and the muscle of his jaw ticked against his cheek.

"I will sleep outside this night." He studied her face. "There is too much at risk, Sarah."

She knew in her heart that he spoke the truth, yet she could not ignore the fire that coursed through her at his kiss.

He carefully returned her hand to her lap and stood.

She attempted to avert her eyes from the bulge beneath the deerskin trousers.

"I will be outside."

"Must you leave? It will be cold." She didn't want to plead, though her very words gave her away.

"For tonight. Tomorrow, I will take you to get the child and then plan a way to get you to the camp."

A piece of Sarah's heart broke at his immediate and certain dismissal. Did all men have the innate ability, in general, to regulate their passions so blithely? Were emotions not involved at all with what lay below the belly?

"I think it is a wise choice as well. We are adults, and as such we should be able to control our passions." She straightened her shoulders, stiffening her jaw. It was the only means of saving her dignity.

His knowing gaze captured hers, deflating any contrived resolve.

"I'll be fine alone." She tossed him a blanket that his sister had left.

White Eagle reached out and caught it with one hand. "Sleep well." He disappeared through the narrow opening into the pitch black.

Sleep, she doubted would come to her at all this night.

CHAPTER ELEVEN

Dangerous Moon

The plunge into the darkness of the frigid river helped somewhat to quell the flames of desire Sarah fanned in him.

White Eagle gazed up at the velvet night sky dusted with a million glittering stars. It did him good to get out of the cave, away from the torment of Sarah's presence to his primitive urges. Her scent lingered in his mind, as did the blatant desire she'd tried to hide from him.

Blinking his eyes from her sultry image, he focused instead on how best to sneak her near enough to the camp that she would be safe going the rest of the way without him. He knew if he were seen they would arrest him and put him in one of the stockades being built with alarming rate in the white settlements.

And yet there stood another danger—Tsula and his men. If they knew she'd survived the attack and were en route to a camp, there was no way of knowing what they might do to her.

The image of Isabella in Sarah's arms flitted into his thoughts and he smiled. For not being a true mother, she was very good with the child—at least as good as any mother with limited resources.

A low chuckle erupted under his breath as he wondered what she must have thought while they discussed her milk supply. His fingers tingled at the mental picture

of her breasts straining against the thin white cotton of
her blouse. She would make a fine mother one day, he reasoned in silence. No doubt she would marry a soldier or
a statesman, perhaps one who would give her the life she
was accustomed to.

He closed his eyes, hoping sleep would dispel the urges
of his heart and his body, instead, he dreamt of Sarah and
of the life they might have had if fate had cast different
lots.

Together they would gather what they needed for each
day. Long summer afternoons spent with their children,
teaching them about mother earth and the bounty of her
existence. And nights filled with Sarah's hushed sighs and
gentle hands.

In his dream she appeared to him bathed in the moonlight, her arms outstretched and skin glittering with the
radiance of the moon.

He reached for her as she lowered herself to him covering his body like a warm breeze across a meadow. She
offered him a hundred kisses, allowing him to sample the
same of her neck, taking his time as he followed the gentle slope of her pale shoulder. He tasted the sweetness of
the valley between her breasts and felt her tremble at his
touch. Her hands, small, but sure, stroked his face, as her
sighs did the same for him, bringing his heart to a fevered
pitch.

His body floated from desperate yearning to an ethereal bliss. At her touch, she commanded him, her dark
hair brushing over his chest setting fire in its wake. Cradled astride his hips, she held her arms high embracing
her moonlit gown, welcoming him, bidding him freedom
from his fear. His life, his breath hung on her every plea-

sured sigh. With her smile she gazed at him, lifting her face to the heavens, blessing his torment, and releasing him from his self-imposed bondage. In one shattering moment he broke free. His fears, his heart, his very soul poured out of him, given wholly to the one woman who could never be his.

White Eagle awoke, drenched in sweat, his body tight with need. Around him the night breezes blew a welcome relief to his heated emotions.

A shrill screech of a hawk in the night sky, much too close for coincidence, caused his ears to pique, waiting for the confirmation of another sound.

A twig snapped and he got to his feet, keeping low in the shadows. He crept to a large boulder near the cave entrance. In the light of the moon on the trail, he could see the Indian pressed against the outer cave wall, carefully picking his way to the entrance. From his movement, it was evident that the he knew where he was going and most likely what he sought. However, it was just as clear he did not know the terrain as well as two people—himself and Tsula. The renegade warrior must know he had the woman and the child or else why send a scout to check out a place that only the two of them knew about?

The intruder crept closer and as he glanced over his shoulder, White Eagle took his advantage and leapt toward the man. A look of surprise met him as his body slammed against the stranger sending them both sprawling over dirt and loose rock.

The ridge not more than a few feet from the entrance held a drop of more than thirty-five feet through the branches of tall pine trees. For two young boys, the feature was an aid to roaming bears. To one not aware, the drop could prove deadly.

Favoring his shoulder, White Eagle struggled with the invader. Though roughly the same size, the man possessed two good arms and the strength of good health. Combined with determination, White Eagle's impairment provided a sluggish match for his opponent.

Thrown to the ground, White Eagle felt pain sear through his shoulder and he grabbed his arm to protect it from further assault. In the next instant, the man attacked him from above and with a warrior's instinct; White Eagle raised his legs, catching the prowler in the chest. With as much force as he could muster, he catapulted the unwelcome guest over his head.

He heard the muffled thud of his body hit the ground and turned quickly to his stomach preparing to rise to his feet to confront his attacker. He only hoped that Sarah was asleep or would not be so curious as to wander outside.

In the still of the night, White Eagle heard a scratching noise, almost desperate like a trapped animal clawing his way out. He stood, poised ready for the next attack, his gaze darting at the shadows around him, but he could not see any movement.

A man's scream sliced the quiet, quelled by a dull thump and then all was still once more, the forest claiming another to its untamed strength.

White Eagle's eyes widened as he realized what had happened. By the time he reached the edge of the drop, there was nothing to meet him but the disturbing quiet.

"Mr. White Eagle?"

His heart still erratic from his fight for survival he stepped quickly toward Sarah and grabbed her arm, pulling her against the shelter of a tree.

"I heard—"

"Sshhh." He covered her mouth with his hand and held his head to listen for further movement around them. Would Tsula be foolish enough to send a man alone? His thoughts ran together, calculating the time and distance of how far behind Tsula and his men might be.

His heart slowed when no other sound, save that of the forest at night could be heard. He knew a man lay at the bottom of the cliff, but there was little he could do for him now. Still, he would get Sarah back inside and check for himself.

It was then he realized his body was pressed against hers, pinning her back to the tree. He slowly dropped his hand from her mouth, but was unwilling to move from the touch of her heartbeat against his. The need to protect her at all costs went beyond his rational. She was a woman after all, and a white woman as well. Her chances of survival traveling through this territory filled with so much unrest would be—at best—minimal. He reminded himself of this as he cautiously stepped away from her.

"There was someone here." It was not a question, but a statement and one he would not deny. She would have to know he'd most likely killed a man.

"There was one, an Indian scout." He hesitated.

"Are there others do you think?" She stepped toward him, peering over his shoulder. Unafraid, she rested her hand on his forearm.

"I do not think there are others now, but more are not far behind." The scent of her hair held him close for a moment before he stepped away again.

"This arrangement is silly. There is no reason we can't

both sleep near the warmth of the fire." She took a step toward him and though her expression was indiscernible, her very presence affected him in puzzling ways.

Her impatient sigh brought his attention back to her face.

"You might catch something out here in this damp night air and that would not bode well for your shoulder."

He arched a brow, unsure that her suggestion would bode well for his sanity. "This is not wise, Sarah."

She placed her hands on her hips. "Well, we'll just have to be wise then, won't we? No more of this nonsense now, follow me. The fire has warmed the cave nicely." She stepped around him, her skirts whirling in the dirt causing stones to skitter across the ground.

He did follow, though against his better judgment given the vision he'd just dreamed.

"You sleep over there on your pallet." She pointed to his bed of straw. "I'll sleep here." The commanding tone of her sharp tongue made him smile. She might look fragile, but she had much spirit.

He watched her frantically fluffing the straw of her bed and shoved back the thought that her spirit might be a cover for desire.

"Do you think we are still safe here?" Her gaze darted to the cave entrance.

Realizing that his bed was to the back of the cave he bent down, touching her shoulders and she stiffened. "You sleep in back I will sleep near the entrance."

Without argument she stood, and did not look at him as she brushed past him to exchange beds.

It was apparent she was not as emotionally affected as he by the occurrences between them earlier. White Eagle reassessed his purpose, reminding himself that in a few days what happened here would be but a memory.

"Do you think they will come again tonight?" She lay on her pallet, tucking her crumpled jacket beneath her head. A strand of her dark hair caught at the edge of her mouth and he wanted to reach out and brush it aside.

"You have nothing to fear. This was a scout. This tells me Tsula and his men are a day or more ride from here." That was his fervent hope anyway.

"Tsula is the man who killed Laura and Captain McKenna." Her eyes searched his for answers.

White Eagle remained standing as he glanced at her. "The attack was meant only to frighten. He did not plan on killing anyone."

"As you did not plan on killing that man out there?"

He had not spoken of the incident, hoping she would think the man had run off.

"No, that also was not planned." He sighed. "Nor could it be helped."

He wanted to explain to her the Cherokee code which called for restitution of life for life, but he feared she would think him barbaric. Many Cherokee had been brutally beaten, some killed in the progress of white settlements searching for the gold the Indians had discovered in the eastern states. Cherokee code, and refusing to leave without a fight, is what spurned Tsula on.

"I know you were only protecting yourself." She turned her gaze to his. "And me. Thank you, again."

To have her recognize and praise his efforts only heightened his awareness that he wanted to always protect her. What was it about this woman that could command his very emotions?

"I must go check the base of the ridge." He glanced at her as she shifted, drawing her hand up to rest it under her cheek. His gaze held to her hand wishing it was his.

"He must be brought to justice, this fellow named Tsula." She blinked, trying to keep her eyes open.

White Eagle stared at her through the flickering firelight. "Justice will be served, Sarah, but perhaps, not as you think it should." The chasm of their cultural differences grew greater as they held each other's gaze. It reminded him once again how important it was to get his emotions under control.

"I will be outside for just a moment. Try to sleep."

As he made his way to the base of the ridge, White Eagle realized that he would need to keep his mind clear in order to get Sarah and Isabella back to their people safely.

He found the scout, his body contorted in such a way that it was evident he'd died from a break to his neck in the fall. Carefully shifting the body, White Eagle gathered leaves and branches, covering him to avoid the woodland creatures scavenging for food. Saying a prayer for his soul and for the Great Spirit to give him wisdom with this woman, he turned and walked back to the cave.

He had no idea if she was awake or not when he returned. "We will leave at daybreak. It will be necessary to stay ahead of Tsula and his men."

She yawned, placing a dainty hand over her mouth, "Did I tell you that I know boxing?"

"Boxing?" She continued to surprise him.

"Fighting with your fists, Mr. White Eagle. Our housemother, Miss Clara taught Emily and me." She held up a doubled fist, shaking it weakly. "I can defend myself if the situation warrants."

He smiled picturing Sarah in hand-to-hand combat.

"A most helpful attribute and one I shall remember." He refrained from wanting to lean over and kiss her knuckles.

"I just didn't want you to think me fragile, Mr. White Eagle. Pleasant dreams." She shifted as he lay down on his pallet.

On the contrary, in many ways she had as much stamina as he. It made her all the more appealing.

He lay awake for some time, memorizing every curve of her back, the way her dark hair fell over one shoulder revealing the soft corkscrew curls at the base of her neck. Her arms, now bare of sleeves torn for bandages and rags, peeked above the brown blanket, contrasting her pale skin.

White Eagle watched her until the fire dwindled and he could barely discern the gentle rise and fall of her shoulder in slumber.

Only then was he able to close his eyes.

Tsula bolted upright, awakened by his disturbing dream. He wiped the sweat from his brow and brought his heart to a steady beat. His gaze quickly scanned the group of sleeping men around the now cold campfire. The full autumn moon splayed a brilliant luster to the forest clearing where they'd set up camp.

"Something troubles you, Tsula?" The Shaman who'd joined the band of renegades for spiritual direction rubbed the sleep from his eyes.

Tsula glanced at the moon. How many nights had he spent beneath its yellow embrace, in this land he called home?

"A dream disturbs my sleep." He pushed his hands over his face trying to dispel the image of White Eagle's face contorted in pain.

"These are disturbing days in which we now live." The Shaman sighed.

Tsula nodded his agreement. The scout he'd sent a day ago to the secret cave, known only to himself and White Eagle, had not yet returned.

He stared at the moon. Perhaps he was delayed, or perhaps he'd run into White Eagle. Tsula had seen how he'd pulled the woman and child to safety just as the wagon toppled into the ravine, but in all the confusion that ensued, he had lost track of his friend until later when they confronted each other about the attack. The arrow was meant to detour White Eagle long enough to gather what remained of his men and reach a safe place where they could regroup. Was it possible he could be protecting this woman and her child still?

He knew he could find out from his Cherokee confident on the inside of the fort. His connection claimed to know this Reynolds man very well, yet remained staunchly loyal to the Cherokee cause. Tsula knew that Chief John Ross and his delegation were still attempting to use legislation to delay the powerful government machine already rolling over many Cherokee tribes.

Rumors of arrests, and suffocating detainment camps spread like wildfire through the villages. Many had already succumbed to the bribes the white government offered, but he would not accept their useless paper promises. This was his home and the home of his fathers before him, and he would not allow any white man to intimidate him.

Tomorrow, he would follow the scout's path and would send word to the fort to speak with his spy. Perhaps he could find the list of the settlers who were on the wagon train. There had to be a good reason why White Eagle would risk his life to protect a white woman and her child.

CHAPTER TWELVE

Whisper On the Wind

White Eagle's moans during the night had not escaped Sarah. Early, while the moon still shone in the morning sky, she lay awake watching him. His restless sleep disturbed her more than she cared to admit and she hoped he would be strong enough to make the two-day journey.

There was little to do in way of preparing to leave other than gather those few possessions she'd tucked in her pockets and the clothing on her back. She stared at her journal, turning it over in her hands and pondered what Emily would think of her adventures thus far. Her lovely once royal blue riding jacket lay crumpled in a heap on the floor, threads hanging from where stone and branches had plucked at its brocade needlework. Her locket, attached to the long gold chain, she had used as a bookmark in her journal. That was all she had and yet she'd survived, not in the comfort she was accustomed to, but with ingenuity and independence she hadn't known she possessed.

Sarah glanced at White Eagle who now slept in peaceful repose, his smooth, muscular chest rising and falling in steady rhythm. Her gaze drifted dreamily to where he'd placed her hand.

"I trust you are well rested, Sarah?" He had not yet opened his eyes.

Her cheeks warmed from embarrassment.

White Eagle turned his head then and opened his eyes,

studying her.

Suddenly she realized she needed fresh air, to say nothing of needing to put a greater distance between herself and White Eagle.

"I'll take these outside." She stuffed her journal in her satchel and stood to leave.

"We travel far today. It will be best to be comfortable on our journey." The tone of his voice made her curious, causing her to pause. She knew there was but one horse.

"We can simply take turns walking." She shrugged as she glanced back, finding him adjusting his breeches. Sarah quickly averted her gaze.

"To find me interesting to look at is not wrong, Sarah."

Her mouth dropped open, aghast at his blatancy. "I—"

"Is it unusual for white women to speak of their desires?"

"Um, well," her tongue failed along with her brain. Such subjects were still considered taboo amongst those in proper circles, to say nothing of being alone in the company of a strange man.

"It is not so with women of my tribe. Cherokee women are free to express their passion. It is what keeps our people strong. Did you know it is our custom for the woman to choose her husband?"

Sarah shook her head no, swallowing at the constriction in her throat. Stranger or not, was he implying she was not passionate? Given the right situation—*the proper situation*—she was certain she could be as passionate and fiery as any woman—White or Cherokee. She almost told him as much right then, but thought it best to let it go. "I believe it would be wise for us to be on our way."

"I am trying to make you see, Sarah. You and I are

different from each other in many ways. Your people have strange ideas—"

"More so than your people?" She retaliated. If he wanted passion she would give him passion. Her ire prickled just below the surface.

"They are different, as are your customs from mine." He paused; stepping around the gray dredges of the campfire, and stood before her. "You are safe in knowing that I will not harm you, nor will I force myself on you."

For the most part, she knew she should feel relieved at his direct statement.

White Eagle stooped to flick the ashes with a stick, making to cover the warm embers. He glanced up at her, "My people, some, not all, are not so different from some white men, Sarah. They would not accept you into our clan any more than your people would accept me." He dropped the stick and stood gazing at her, his dark eyes intent. "So you see nothing will happen between us that can change who we are or where we belong."

She knew deep in her heart, he was right, yet why did her insides quiver every time he was within two feet of her?

"It will be best to know these things before we begin our journey together."

She licked her lips, frowning in an effort to control the emotions skittering around, openly taunting her better sense. The image of her father's face, purple with rage, swam in her memory, followed by Laura's lifeless gaze. Those easily quelled any passion smoldering in her being.

"Yes, of course. Thank you for reminding me." She blinked, returning her attention to his steady gaze. Better she should place all things in perspective now, it would make things much easier down the road. Casting her silly romantic notions behind, she turned, carefully avoiding the low ceiling and did not look back.

Sarah would remind herself several times of his words that morning. She would ignore the flicker of desire that flashed in his dark eyes as he lifted her to the horse. He'd insisted she ride in front, stating his concern was for her safety should Tsula come upon them from the rear. The reality however of possible attack, did not affect her as much as the secure reality of his strong arms draped loosely around her. No, a much greater fear had arisen inside her. Something that even her book knowledge could not quell. This fear held her stomach tight and scattered her reason beyond the wind. It appeased itself only in random thoughts and wishful musings and she knew if caught in its clutches, her heart would be torn in two.

She was falling in love with White Eagle and worse than the division of their race, was the divide he'd already created of his own accord. The thought was insane. To entertain the idea that a man of his passion and stature within a tribe that held him in high regard could ever have feelings for her, none that would have any longevity at any rate, was clearly without sound sense. It was evident that she should clear her mind of such fanciful thoughts.

She sat straight, taking note of the scenery around them. At least *this* was tangible, *this* she could write down and look back upon without regret. *This* she could use to cover the desperate loneliness inside her at the thought of never seeing him again.

"It is beautiful here." Sarah scanned the wooded area beyond the trail. The sun's rays sliced through the feathery branches of leaves creating a rippled effect of light that played hopscotch with the shadows of the forest floor.

The gentle thud of the horse's hooves slapped against the mossy grass and the scent of pine, mingled with that of White Eagle's skin. She knew the smell would forever hold more than the memory of Christmas boughs and evergreen roping.

It would remind her of him. He embodied the earth, in all its strength, wonder, and passion. In all that was good and true, White Eagle already represented these things in her heart.

He'd not responded, but she knew he'd heard her. The warmth of his breath tickled the back of her neck and she trembled.

"Are you cold, Sarah?" His low timbered voice coaxed yet another unexpected shiver from her.

Remembering his words, she shifted her shoulders, sitting taller. "I'm fine." She hesitated hoping it sounded like the truth, then added for good measure, "It's the thought of meeting those horrid men that sends chills up my spine."

Several moments passed as Sarah waited for some type of response, but all she heard was the shrill call of a whip-poorwill.

After quite some time, he spoke, "You need not fear, Sarah. I will protect you. Once we have the child from my people, then I myself will make sure you get to the camp. There you will be safe; though I hope you will take caution and return to where you came from. This land is not safe as it once was."

There was so much she wanted to ask him about the way things used to be. She wanted to know more about him, his family, his tribe, yet another part of her wanted to ask why he cared if she should stay or leave.

Another part of her fought a disappointment threatening to break forth into tears. Foolish as the romantic notions about him were, she could not deny the fact she was attracted to him in many ways. He possessed honor and respect for the earth that she found appealing in a chivalrous way. She immediately stopped her voluntary review of his attributes with the onset of the tingling in the pit of her stomach.

"We will camp here near the river, tonight." Without discussion he veered the horse toward a clearing surrounded by pines. He slid from the appaloosa, agile in his descent and landing.

Leaning her body forward, Sarah tugged her leg over the broad back of the horse and dropped to the ground only to have her legs buckle from beneath her. Perhaps it had been longer than she thought since she'd ridden at great lengths.

"I have no sensation in my legs." The fact mystified her since she considered herself a fine equestrian. Granted that was also sidesaddle.

"It will be well." White Eagle gave an amused chuckle. "Walk around and the blood will return to your legs."

Perhaps there were more things that men—white or Cherokee—in general had in common to one another. Say for instance, their maddening penchant for thinking highly of themselves.

"I never doubted that, Mr. White Eagle." She labored to her knees, pausing with her hand to the horse's belly, gaining the strength to continue to her feet. Glancing up, she caught his perplexed gaze, his arms folded over his chest as though waiting for her to request his help.

In a pig's eye.

Searching around her, she spied a thick branch and

grabbed it, hoisting herself upright with its aid. Brushing her skirts, she held his challenging gaze.

White Eagle shook his head, then plucked the reins from the horses back, and led him through the trees.

"Where are you going?" Her gaze snagged on the muscles rippling along his back as he walked away.

"To the river, the horse needs water." he called over his shoulder. "You are welcome to join us."

Welcome? "Thank you, I'll be along shortly." Sarah shook one leg and then the other as she braced herself against the branch. She glanced up, holding her skirt in one hand above her ankles and watched his departing form.

"Do not take long. There are many wild animals in the woods."

She made a quick scan around her, realizing that if she did not follow she would soon be standing on the trail alone.

Sarah paused at the river's edge, far enough from the man and his horse drinking side by side. Carefully eyeing the green river, she bent down and scooped her hand into the cool water, taking sip after sip of its refreshing taste. Rubbing the water over her cheeks, she longed to simply jump in.

She found herself glancing at White Eagle and the gentle way he cared for the steed, and was surprised at the snippet of jealousy that appeared in her mind.

Turning her thoughts quickly, she studied the shoreline across the river. Fall did not turn the leaves as quickly here as it did in New York, but the shimmer of the setting sun glowed red on the river causing it to sparkle. At a time when she should be anxious and fearful, a calm serenity pervaded her senses making her all the more aware of the beauty around her. How much she'd missed by living in the city all those years.

"I will find us some food. Will you be able to gather wood for a fire?" He led the horse to a tree, looping the reins over a branch.

"I think I can do that." She placed her hand on one hip, hoping he would see her displeasure in his apparent lack of faith in her abilities. "I am not as helpless as you must think, Mr. White Eagle."

White Eagle walked toward her, though she swore it was more of a swagger really, perhaps only the imagination of a weary mind.

He held a steady gaze to hers as he brushed by her shoulder. "I never doubted it, Miss Sarah."

Later she would ponder whether it was his condescending tone, or his wicked smile that mocked her.

She narrowed her gaze at the river, tempted to pick up a stone and haul it at his back. Instead Sarah decided to wait until after nightfall and cool off her emotions by taking a leisurely swim in the river.

She'd be damned if she would let him get to her.

CHAPTER THIRTEEN

Two Faced Messenger

Tsula handed the list back to the silent Indian. Except for the color of his skin, one would not have guessed by his polished attire that he was an Indian. He'd done well in serving both white man and Cherokee as a messenger for both sides.

"You are certain she was not among those brought in?" Tsula clasped his hands behind his back as he slowly paced in front of the man. If what this two-faced spy told him was the truth, it could bode well as much needed good news for his mission.

"It was verified. Sarah Reynolds and a child, an infant, were not accounted for. The infant's parent's, however were among those killed in the attack."

Tsula did not wish to be reminded of the mistakes his men had made that fateful day. "And you are certain she is the daughter of Charles Reynolds?"

The man pressed fresh tobacco into the new pipe he'd been given after a full meal of venison and corn. "The captain had not spoken of a daughter, but when her name was mentioned, he had an odd look in his eye." The man nodded, puffing to bring his smoke to life, "It is his daughter, I am certain."

Tsula eyed the man contented in smoking his pipe. There was no reason to fear he was not telling the truth. The man knew fully the risk he took in offering both sides important information. To have Sarah Reynolds as a bargaining tool would certainly gain their advantage over the ruthless Reynolds and his men.

Just that morning had confirmed any suspicions that White Eagle did not travel alone. When they'd arrived at the cave, there'd been two pallets and any further proof they needed was found at the base of the ridge with the discovery of the scout's body. Evidence that White Eagle was defending himself or someone else.

Tsula stared at the messenger of this latest, most revealing news and wondered if White Eagle was aware he harbored the daughter of the man who'd terrorized their people. "Perhaps White Eagle will see now the necessity of our mission," Tsula spoke his thoughts aloud.

"Excuse me? *White Eagle?* Does he have something to do with Sarah Reynolds?" The man drew his pipe from his lips, his gaze keenly narrowed on Tsula.

A sudden distaste formed in his stomach for the man seated before him. "No, it is someone I am to meet tomorrow. That is all." Tsula leaned forward placing his hand on the man's shoulder. "You have done well. Leave the rest to me." He offered the man a friendly smile, but in his mind the sooner the man left the better.

Tsula summoned one of his men to bring the messenger's horse. "Be careful, my friend." He studied the man, wondering what his future would hold.

His gaze followed the man only for a moment as he galloped away from the camp, then he turned to his second in command. "We will ride under cover of darkness. There is someone I wish to meet by morning's light."

The man nodded, and began barking out orders in their native tongue. Tsula only half-listened, his thoughts absorbed in how to convince White Eagle to join them, especially now. They could use a man with his sharp skills, but if White Eagle persisted in his resistance to their mission then he would do what he needed to in order to save his people and free them from the fear of the white man.

The woman was driving White Eagle to the brink of lunacy. All day he'd ridden, fitting all too comfortably against her backside, enduring the scent of her hair in his face, and the gentle brush of her body to his.

He prayed as he readied his bow, asking the Great Spirit to aid him in finding a plump rabbit or squirrel. At the same time, he prayed for wisdom to help him see the folly of what his heart was slowly revealing to him. He cared for this woman—deeply.

Sweat formed at his temple as he set his sight on a rabbit seated at the base of a tree nibbling grass. Silently he stretched his bow, pulling the arrow to his shoulder with keen precision. Narrowing one eye he focused on the animal, zeroing in on his exact target. A flash of a tempting image revealed Sarah's smile in his dream as she released herself to him. He blinked and in the same instant his finger slipped, sending the arrow flying far from its intended mark.

Frustration pummeled White Eagle and he closed his eyes as he heard the dull thump of the arrow hitting the tree. With a flicker of hope he opened them just in time to see the rabbit scurry back into its lair. His patience pulled tight, he ground his teeth, seething in his lack of control over his emotions when it came to her. He'd not meant to find himself in this predicament. He'd only seen her and the child and could not abide letting Tsula's men slaughter them as they'd done to the others. If he'd had more time, he might have saved others, but that was put an end when Tsula pulled his bow and shot him. In White Eagle's eyes, there would be few ways to reason with Tsula and his men now.

It was several hours later before he returned with a small squirrel. Many of his arrows he would have to find in the morning, this meager offering he was able to kill with a stone.

"Were you successf—" her words halted as her gaze dropped to the scrawny squirrel hanging from his belt. Sarah lifted her eyes in horror as if to say he should assure her this was *not* their supper.

"Winter is coming, animals are scarce." He hoped she would not prolong his humiliation much more than he'd already exercised on himself. It was not the first time he'd been untruthful with her.

"Perhaps there are fish?" She checked over her shoulder toward the river, pointing with her thumb, before returning her attention to the dead animal.

Maybe this was not the time to tell her how valuable squirrel hide was. "You are most welcome to try your luck with the river. I will skin this and place it over the fire." He pulled the carcass from his belt and slapped it on the other end of the log where she sat.

She bolted from the log and stared first at the animal, then at him. It was plain to see she had never experienced hunting for food.

"Sarah." He stabbed the point of his knife in the wood and she jumped. "Squirrel meat is a delicacy for some people. Its' taste is not all that different from what you eat."

Her pallor did not convince him that he'd calmed her fears.

"I believe I will go down to the river while you," she waved her hand towards the carcass, "do what you need to do."

White Eagle nodded as held up his knife, checking the edge for sharpness. He kept his focus on the blade. "Be watchful. There are animals that come to the river to drink at night." He glanced askew at Sarah, knowing that he should not taunt her in this way, yet he'd come to enjoy watching the fire blaze behind her eyes. He knew it was a dangerous game he played.

"I shan't wander." She narrowed her gaze at him.

He turned back to his task, his heart peaceful in that knowledge.

"Emily, if I could wish for one thing it would be for your thoughts on this man," Sarah spoke tersely as she shirked off her blouse and riding skirt, stripping down to her camisole and slip. She lifted the edge, noting the uneven hem, where she'd torn the cotton for bandages. The night breeze was chilly, but still warm for fall and she stood for a moment gazing on the reflection of the yellow harvest moon on the dark, glassy river.

A southerly wind whispered gently through the leaves, and she closed her eyes, trying to sort out her tangled thoughts. She listened to the chorus of crickets chirping their shrill call as a toad added his heavy croak to the song.

With caution, she tested the temperature of the water, wading out waist deep until it welcomed her, enveloping her in its still darkness. The cool rush of water slid over her emotions, as it glided sensuously over her skin. Pausing in the deep part of the river, she pushed back the hair from her face and searched the bank. At a distance through a patch of bushes, she could see White Eagle hard at work, preparing the squirrel. This was normal; it was his way of life. Logically she should understand it and yet she realized she bore many prejudices, too much of what she'd seen and heard in the past few days.

Long strands of moss licked at her legs as she treaded water and she recalled with sudden urgency his last warning. Diving in, she swam toward the bank, but her thoughts returned to the days' journey and despite their differences of culture, how right it felt to be next him.

She reached the sandy bar at the river's edge and grasped hold of a large boulder, pulling herself to sit on its surface. Dragging her sodden hair to the side, she twisted it through her hands, wringing the excess water free, tossing it over her shoulder. Refreshed from the swim, she allowed her thoughts and emotions to flutter into place, trying to make sense where there was none and trying to rationalize the tugging taking precedence in her heart.

She thought of her father and wondered if he was looking for her. She also questioned the dealings of this man, Tsula, and what would prompt him to attack an innocent group of people. Though she knew White Eagle had lent no part in the attack, she wanted to ask if he knew why it had taken place at all.

As she stared at the full harvest moon, the wind dried her hair, causing it to tickle her chilling arms. Yet the shiver it produced was the same enticing, ripple that snaked over her skin each time she was near White Eagle.

Sarah stretched back on the rock, staring up at the stars. With a sigh of release she let her memory drift to when he'd kissed her in the cave. How her body had quickened when he'd slid his strong arm around her, drawing it solidly against the warmth of his chest. She remembered his fevered kiss seeking fulfillment, and their breath, in soft, whispered sighs indicating without words their desire for more. Engulfed in her thoughts, her body reacted of its own accord, surprising her to the deeper desires she held inside.

A twig snapped underfoot of something or someone, bringing Sarah upright as she listened again for additional sounds.

"Mr. White Eagle?" Fear held its icy hands to her throat so tight her words were barely audible.

A low growl emitted from the darkness nearby and she considered standing atop the rock and screaming for White Eagle. Instead, she feared that whatever was there might also harm him. Perhaps if she could get close enough without being seen she could frighten it away. She stepped delicately from the boulder into the ankle deep water cautiously tiptoeing over the sand and rock bottom. Still she was not more than a foot from the bank.

As she rounded the thigh high bushes near the water's edge, she heard a low rumbling growl accompanied by a gentle lapping at the water. Sarah froze in place as she came face-to-face with a bear.

She could not move, nor could she scream. It was difficult for her to focus on the animal's size despite her several attempts to do so. In the dark, all she could determine was he was on all fours, thirsty and did not wish to be disturbed.

He lapped at the water, and then paused, lifting his head to meet her fearful gaze as though he'd just realized her presence.

Sarah wanted to open her mouth, her mind begged her to do so, but every muscle in her body had gone rigid.

Suddenly the beast turned, giving a disgruntled growl and stood on its hind legs.

Her heart pounded hard against her chest and her gaze darted to the crest of the embankment where she knew just out of sight, White Eagle cooked their evening meal.

If she could smell the scent of roasting meat, then surely so would this ferocious beast.

Perhaps by throwing rocks at it, she could scare him off. She glanced around, unable to detect anything but the dark water swirling at her ankles.

A short, high-pitched yelp from the bear riveted her attention back to shore and she noted, with great relief, the bear loping away through the trees.

Relief besieged her and she grabbed her cotton skirt, wading quickly to the bank, stopping dead in her tracks as she confronted the reason for the bear's immediate retreat.

A large snake, his pale olive skin glittering in the moonlight blocked her way of escape.

With thoughts of outrunning him, she turned; hoping to make it to the boulder, but the snake lashed out and the stab of his fangs sank into the soft flesh of her foot. Pain summoned the scream from her throat and then chaos erupted around her.

White Eagle appeared on the bank and grabbing a rock, slammed it over the snake's head.

His image swayed before her eyes as he came towards

her and she sensed his arms go around her as the world upended.

Sarah awoke some time later, groggy, but aware that the left side of her body was warm. A strange sensation tugged at the skin of her foot and she glanced down to see White Eagle kneeling at her feet appearing from what she could determine, to be nibbling on her instep.

While the sensation held a grain of euphoric pleasure, her body was too weak to appreciate it in full. She pressed her memory to recall the events leading her back to the campfire.

"What happened?" The image of him raising the rock above his head and smashing against the ground swam in her muddled thoughts.

He continued his task without looking at her. She could feel his teeth pressing hard against the flesh of her foot, and the suction tugging against his lips.

His rough hand slid over her calf, pressing the muscle causing her to jump.

"Can you feel your legs?"

She thought by her reaction that much should be obvious. "Yes, but—"

"And your arms?" he interrupted; pausing long enough to grab her hand and jiggle her arm until she thought it would fall off.

"Yes, if you'd—"

He hovered over her a moment, then dropped his head to her chest as though listening.

"What are—" Her impatience found contentment in his concern, but too quickly he rose, rocking back on his heels.

"Your heartbeat is steady. That is a good sign."

"A sign?" Her memory then came full alert, remembering the pain of the bite. "Was the snake that bit me poisonous?"

"A cotton-mouth." He rested his hands on his thighs and frowned at her foot. His dark eyes assessed her slowly from head to toe and she was certain if he'd checked her now he'd definitely find an erratic heartbeat.

"I do not think you gained much of the poison. If this were so, you would not have the use of your arms and legs." He picked up her hand more gently this time and rubbed his thumb over the back of her fingers.

Sarah stared at him, and then the thought occurred to her. "Maybe he bit the bear first."

"The bear?" He turned, his brows furrowed in question.

Sarah nodded, swallowing the dry lump in her throat, "Yes, when I came around the bushes, there was a bear drinking in the river. He rose up on his legs and yelped as though he was in pai—" It occurred to her then that the snake had probably bitten the bear as well.

White Eagle's shoulders relaxed and a shadow of a smile played at the corner of his mouth.

"What?" The man was the most puzzling human being she'd ever met.

"You will live, Sarah. The bear, I'm afraid, may not. He took the greatest share of the venom."

For a moment, she actually felt sorry for the animal. "So once again, it appears I am indebted to you for my life."

He closed his eyes turning his face to the sky.

Whatever it was he was doing, instinct cautioned her to remain silent.

The popping crackle of the campfire sounded near her ear as she watched him in the flickering light. He was an enigma, this man, more gracious and kind than many educated white men, yet primal in his view of life.

Without a word, he scooped her into his arms, adjusting her until she lay cradled comfortably against him. Her heart beat fierce as her thin clothing permitted even the heat of his hands to touch her skin.

"Where are you taking me?"

White Eagle turned, edging down the embankment. "To wash out the wound left from the cut."

"The cut?" She lifted her foot trying to turn her ankle for a better look.

"From my knife."

Sarah's eyes widened. "The same one you used on that *dead* creature?"

They neared the riverbank and the grass sloshed underfoot as he waded into the water. "The squirrel was clean."

CHAPTER FOURTEEN

Ransom Current

White Eagle's emotions swirled with confusion, both quelled promptly as he plopped Sarah's backside on the unrelenting hardness of the boulder.

"What are—"?

"Place your ankle in the water."

"I'm too high."

He stepped back assessing the situation briefly, then grabbed her slip and flung it over her knees. "Then you will come forward."

Wadding her skirt in her hand she scooted forward, inching as she stretched her foot towards the water.

"More," he commanded. Not hiding his frustration, he stepped forward and unashamedly grabbed her backside pulling her forward.

With a soft squeal of surprise, she lost her balance, nearly toppling over the side, instead she slammed smack into his chest—though her foot now dangled in the water.

Had he noticed the whisper thin of her cotton camisole before now? White Eagle focused on her wound, trying desperately to avoid the sensation of her soft thigh sliding against his leg.

Her eyes, at close proximity glittered like onyx in the moonlight.

"Now we will let it stay in the water."

"Very well." Her gaze lowered briefly to his mouth and

then over his shoulder.

She teetered on the edge of the boulder propped up only by the support of his body. It appeared to him that this woman was some sort of odd temperament of the gods sent to challenge him in every way.

As though unsure what to do with her hands, she placed them gingerly around the base of his neck. "I don't want to hurt your shoulder."

"Thank you." He glanced up, not dwelling long on her gaze, refusing to acknowledge the feathery softness of her fingertips on his skin. "Why didn't you call to me instead of trying to fight the snake yourself?"

"I had no idea the snake was there." She shrugged, causing the dainty lace strap of her camisole to list over her shoulder.

He pulled his gaze back to her face. "And what of the bear? Did you plan to fight him?" A knot began to form in the pit of his stomach and he knew it was unwise to be holding her this close.

She glanced down. "I was afraid if I yelled you would come down the hill unprepared and with your arm I—I didn't want to see you get hurt."

The messenger collapsed in the elegant rose tapestry covered chair, an unusual piece in such a rustic setting, yet not so for the required comfort of the man seated before him. The man who'd introduced him to the many benefits of the white man's world.

He fought to catch his breath after the pressing ride he'd just made. The look in Tsula's eyes revealed more than a mere friendliness and he knew it was not wise to tarry in their camp.

"You have done well." The man across the desk tapped his pen to the document he'd been writing to Georgia Governor Gilmer. "Tell me what you know."

The man leaned back then, folding his large hands over his silver and black brocade vest.

The messenger eyed the vest, wondering if he could find information to bargain for one like it. It would go well with his new black suit, recently acquired from the clothes brought in with the wagon train. "He wished to know who was on the list of travelers' with the wagon train." His eyes darted to the glass half-full of whiskey and then returned to the man's cold gaze.

The messenger shifted under his gaze and he sat up full height, more for his own confidence than to intimidate the man. "He was very interested in a traveler by the name of Sarah Reynolds." He waited, watching with keen and practiced awareness the eyes of the stately white man. The man's pupils turned dark as his gaze narrowed, just as he'd suspected they would.

"And?"

"I told him she and an infant were not counted among those brought in."

"Did he mention their whereabouts?"

"No sir," the messenger answered.

He shifted again, nervous to mention what he thought he'd heard Tsula say.

"Is there more?" The man slowly picked up his glass, swirling it as he always did before sipping. He eyed the messenger over the rim.

The Indian's hands curled nervously at his side, clench-ing and unclenching, still hesitant to mention what he

thought he'd heard. Hadn't Tsula denied saying anything? What little good would it do to stir up something without good information to back it up?

"Well? I don't pay you to keep quiet!" he bellowed.

"Tsula mentioned something about White Eagle."

The man sat up straight, his full attention focused on the Indian. "What did he say? Are this woman and the child being held captive by this barbarian?"

The Indian's ire rose and he wanted to remind him of whose company he kept, but one glance of the man's face silenced his tongue. He swallowed his pride; more interested that the man had yet to admit Sarah Reynolds was his daughter.

"He did not say anything more. Though it is in what he did not say that was of greater importance." Feeling as though he had some amount of leverage over the man, the Indian relaxed easing his back against the chair. Perhaps there would be a glass of whiskey offered to him tonight after all.

"Do you have any idea where this White Eagle is? Where he would go?"

The Indian shrugged. All he had to do was follow Tsula and no doubt he would find White Eagle. "I could find out." A small smile played at his lips. There were times when he'd felt a betrayer to his people, but those moments were short lived when he considered it as a means of survival.

"Do it. Find out where this man is and if he is holding this white woman and the child hostage."

"Would we not have heard something by now if White Eagle planned to use this woman as a bargaining tool?" He knew the minute he spoke the words that the implications

were not going to settle well with the wealthy statesman.

Rising from his chair, the man's face blushed in rage. "You find out and if he has harmed one hair on the head of these settlers, he will answer personally to me." The formidable man slammed his hands to the desktop as he leaned over the desk, glaring at him.

The messenger wondered of the man's animosity toward the lone Indian. Hadn't an entire wagon train just been slaughtered? Could one man commit such a violent act with the intent on capturing one woman and her child? No, there was more to this and it would serve him well to tuck the information away to be used at a later time. There would be no shared drinks this night.

"Yes sir." The messenger rose, realizing the back of his shirt was wet with perspiration.

∞

It took but a few brushes of Sarah's soft bare leg against White Eagle's hip to determine that he would need little incentive to follow through with an idea that would surely lead to disaster.

He swallowed; drawing in every bit of strength, giving him a thousand reasons he should walk away, keep his distance.

"How much longer shall I have to soak my foot?" She crooked her arm over his good shoulder and leaned down staring at the water, busily stirring her foot. She had no idea of what she was putting him through.

He blinked, pushing away the haze of lust clouding his mind, determined to gather enough control to get her back to the camp. To do that he must first command his body to move away from her—an idea that had not yet

reached his brain.

"This is enough. I will find coneflower and make you a salve to place on the wound. It will aid in drawing any remaining poison."

She leaned back, placing her hand to his cheek. "What about you? Is there a chance for any residue of poison on your mouth?" Her eyes glittered in moonlight.

In truth, he'd not considered his own safety. "You use your teeth." He wanted to pull from her gaze, cautioning himself that it was not wise to tarry on the tempting shape of her mouth.

"So, there is no danger?" Her fingers drifted gently over his lips.

For no experience with men, this woman for all her innocence, was a powerful temptress. "Sarah," he cautioned, "there is more danger present than you are aware of."

She hesitated, studying his face, as though assessing his words. "You care for me, don't you?"

He could not answer. Unwilling to admit openly what his heart had already told him. The scent of her skin invaded his senses mingling with the cool night air and making him fearful of releasing the truth of his emotions. Here they were alone in the dark, no one knew if they were alive, no one would know—

White Eagle looked away, staring at the dark water hoping she would let it go because, in truth, he realized he could not.

"You do," she reiterated softly.

Releasing a frustrated sigh, he faced her, hoping intimidation would keep her away. "It is true, Sarah, that I care for you. You were an innocent bystander in a slaughter that made no sense, had no purpose. You were there

with the child and when I saw you—" He took a deep breath, then squared his shoulders, summoning his pride. "I couldn't let it happen. It was wrong what they did."

For the first time, a sense of relief washed over him. Glad he'd been there. Glad that he'd admitted to himself, that fate had brought them together. For what little future that prospect held.

She smiled, framing her face with her delicate hands. "I have come to like you, Mr. White Eagle."

He forced his gaze to the ground. More than her young age, her innocent outlook held no concept of the enormous gap between them. "I have grown fond of you, Sarah, but you see the danger there would be in letting our emotions rule over logic."

"You do not believe that." She lifted his chin to meet her gaze. "Any more than I do. You feel something for me as more than just a caretaker. I can see it when you look at me."

Mesmerized, he stalled, trying to gather the courage to stop what should not begin. She was right, of course. He did care for her. The thought of watching her walk into that camp a few days from now twisted at his heart, but nothing either of them could do would change the way things were.

He grabbed her around the waist, shoving her back to the center of the rock.

Squatting to the water, he washed handfuls over his face, swishing it in his mouth, and spitting it out more than a dozen times.

"You think that will help?"

Her soft voice teased his emotions already drawn tight as a bow. He glanced up, seeing her face peering down at

him. She'd crossed her legs, tucking her skirt around her knees—much to his relief.

"It is wise to be sure rather than leave chance to the wind." He realized then that his pants were soaked above his knees and worse he was fully aroused.

She smiled in response.

White Eagle chose to ignore whatever implications her gesture meant.

"We should return to the fire where it is warm." He nodded as he plucked her from the rock, hoping she would not be able to detect his inability to disguise his attraction.

Too late, her eyes widened as they had in the cave, and much to his dismay, she snuggled a little closer.

He could smell the roasting squirrel as they neared the top of the grassy knoll and he hoped her thoughts would be turned toward her stomach.

The sensation of her lips nibbling near his ear stopped him in his tracks. "What are you doing, Sarah Richardson?"

She shifted to gaze at him. Her expression quietly reflected what was on her mind. "Emily said men like that."

He stared at her, unsure if his brain would be able to engage his mouth.

Though the temptation to ask what else Emily taught her flitted through his senses, he blinked, forcing those questions behind.

"Does it not appeal to you?" she asked coyly.

They stood now in the subtle glow of the fire, its shadows making her eyes all the more luminous. His tongue was glued to the roof of his mouth.

"I'd like to thank you again."

Her breath whispered against his cheek, sending a

warning signal straight to his loins.

"You are welcome." He kept his focus on the roasting squirrel, part of him hoping it would catch fire and he would be saved from this moment.

"Properly." She grabbed his chin, turned his face, and covered his mouth with her own.

Every vision he'd dreamt of her exploded in his mind as her fingers slid past his ears grasping handfuls of his hair, drawing him deeper into the kiss.

He jerked away, breaking the passionate kiss. When he could, he sought her gaze, as she slid down his body to stand before him.

Locusts would be less torment than this woman.

He held her at arm's length and spoke through the desire threatening to constrict his throat, "One day, Sarah, you will find someone who will be happy to teach you what I cannot." He dropped his hands swallowing hard to not pull her back into his arms. "It is better for both of us this way."

She tipped her head, narrowing her gaze. "If I were Cherokee, it would be different, would it not? If my skin were brown like Running Doe, then you would not hesitate to let me show you what I feel for you inside." She balled her fist, pounding it softly between her breasts.

He shook his head. "You are young." White Eagle frowned, pushing back the lie meant to diffuse his lust, yet the fierce desire to drop to his knees and sample the sweetness of the valley where her hand rested burned bright in his heart.

"And you aren't?"

"Why must you do this, Sarah? If you were Cherokee, we would announce our betrothal and then there would be a ceremony. There would be…time. Preparation."

"A ceremony, like a wedding?" She dropped her hand, allowing the camisole to blouse, hiding the perfect shape beneath.

His gaze fought its way to her face. "Yes."

"Tell me."

Grateful for anything that would detour her bewitching ways; White Eagle sprang into a lavish description of the traditional Cherokee ceremony, from the courting flute to the actual ceremony. He tried to ignore the intensity of her attention to his every word.

"Show me how it's done."

He swallowed, unsure the idea was wise to be tampered with. "It is not complicated."

"I may never see one. Show me so I may tell my students one day." Her insistent prodding caused him to grab the blankets from the ground.

"The man and woman each wrap themselves in their own blanket. Those used for weddings are blue." He handed Sarah a blanket and watched as she wrapped it around her shoulders, then she smiled at him.

"Go on."

He spoke as he wrapped the blanket around himself. "Then they meet with the Shaman at the ceremonial campfire that has burned and been blessed by the other tribeswomen for over a week."

"Like this?" She stepped forward and offered her hand to his.

Locked to her gaze, he took it, allowing himself to be pulled nearer.

"Then what happens?" She stared up at him, her eyes searching his with interest and something more. Something he would not allow himself to comprehend fully.

He cleared his throat, "The Shaman—"

"That would be similar to a minister or priest?"

He nodded, losing track of his thoughts as he held her gaze.

"Does what?"

"Then," he collected his thoughts, "the two exchange their separate blankets for a single blanket of white."

"Is that a sign of their virginity?" She asked as she let the blanket drop from her shoulders.

"It is more a symbol of their new life together."

Her brow rose. "What comes next?"

"The man and woman wrap themselves together as one in a wedding blanket."

"Like," she stepped forward pulling the edges of his blanket around her, cocooning them snug against one another, "this? Now what?"

Her breath brushed against his chest, causing his heart to hitch.

"They speak their vows of commitment to each other."

"What kind of vows? What does a Cherokee man offer to his bride in terms of wedding vows, Mr. White Eagle?"

His arms now rested on her shoulders, skin touching skin, their bodies radiating heat between them. He kept his gaze focused on the tree behind her.

White Eagle's mind grappled with trying to recall the weddings he'd attended. "There is loyalty and keeping oneself only for the other."

The hardened pebbles of her breasts played havoc against his chest. Her warm hands slid around his waist splaying across his lower back.

"Sarah," he issued a cautionary tone too feeble to believe in himself.

"What else?" She gently snuggled closer.

He drew in a sharp breath as her lips touched his chest. "To care for her all his life and to bring her happiness, children, and a sturdy home."

His hands followed every curve as they slid down her back. He was amazed how right she felt in his arms.

"Lots of children?" she whispered.

He swallowed, his heart beginning to pound a fierce rhythm in his chest. "Yes." He could barely issue the word from his mouth as he brushed his lips across her forehead, drawing in the scent of her hair.

"What comes next?"

Her question pulled him from the bliss of her body next to his. "Then the Shaman blesses them and the ceremony is celebrated until well into the morning by the tribes' people."

"And what of the new bride and her husband? Do they also stay awake all night?" She glanced up at him with a coy smile and knew at that moment, this night would change their lives forever.

"Yes. They celebrate…in private." He found her gaze and his heart let go what smoldered inside. "In a tent constructed and blessed for the wedding night."

"Show me how they celebrate." She moved her hand to the back of his neck, pulling his face to hers, shattering all resistance he'd worked hard to keep between them.

It was not a request, but a gentle demand. One he could no longer fight.

He wanted to consume her, wanted her to be his, not for just this night, but for the rest of their lives. Moving his mouth over hers, the taste of her on his tongue, made him hunger for more. He dropped to his knees in front of her, pressing his face to her

"Sarah, this…it's not—"

"Not now," she whispered following him to the ground. She knelt before him, her trust so clear that he wished their mock ceremony had been real and that the vows they'd made would allow them to love freely as their hearts bid them.

Sarah kept her gaze on his as she began to unfasten the ribbon lacing of her camisole.

White Eagle moved his hand over hers. "What would this woman say to her future husband?"

Her teeth gently pressed over her bottom lip as she fought the smile tugging the corner of her mouth. She took his hand, pressing it over her breast. "I would tell him my heart is, and always will be yours. No matter what happens, no matter where life takes us. No one will ever take the place of you in my soul."

"That man would consider himself most rich in blessings, Sarah." He gently brushed her hand aside, finishing what she'd started, and slipped the camisole down her soft, pale shoulders. He assessed her beauty, even greater than he imagined, combined with the simple admission of her vows.

CHAPTER FIFTEEN

My Sarah

Sarah held his gaze, her body tingling under his heated appraisal. *This was how it feels to be in love.*

"There is a word we have that expresses beauty, *Ugeyu-di*. It means lovely—" His fingers brushed deftly over her hair, sliding down her shoulder, barely touching her flesh as his fingers grazed her breast. "Beyond my greatest dreams."

Sarah's breath caught. His touch ignited something inside, a desire that caused her heart to race, a need she couldn't explain. "Love me now." She held his gaze, able to see the smoldering heat in his dark eyes. "Love me as you would your wife."

He touched his lips to hers, tentatively. His palm closed around one breast, his mouth moving harder over hers. She clung to him, lost in the pleasure he summoned, her need building with each caress.

The blanket slid to the ground and he lowered her atop it, peeling aside her camisole, his mouth leaving a trail of heated kisses down her exposed flesh.

"Would that the gods bless me with you as my wife," his words whispered against her stomach. His hand moved between her thighs, his fingers moving between her legs, the sensation of the cotton fabric of her slip causing a delightful friction.

Sarah battled the sensations, wanting more, wanting to

be set free from the tension building inside her.

"It is good, Sarah. You will see," he whispered, closing his mouth over her breast.

She whimpered, her body losing control. She grabbed his shoulders, feeling his hair cascading over her flesh. Air rushed over her body as he bunched the skirt to gain access to her warmth, one, then two calloused fingers slid into her, moving in such a way that she lost track of all thought. He looked at her then and with a grin, captured her mouth and her heart as her body shattered in a thousand prisms of light.

"White Eagle—" her words cut short by another wave of pleasure rolling through her body. She arched against his hand, her body shuddering once more. ?" *Was this what Emily spoke of? Is this the delicious dance of pleasure between a woman and a man?*

"My heart cherishes the sound of my name on your lips." He whispered, kissing her eyelids, her cheek, and then softly touching her mouth.

"Sarah, tell me to stop." He rose to his knees. "I will walk straight into the river," he grinned, "and I will not return."

Her heart tumbled in her chest. "There's more?" Most certainly, she had fallen in love with this strong, gentle man.

He chuckled quietly. "Yes, my love, we have only started."

She moved her hand over the firm muscle of his chest. "How on earth could I refuse you?"

"You are certain?"

"No." She was honest when she reached for him. "But tonight I am yours, and you are mine."

Blinded to what was proper, urged on by a mystery that delved much deeper than the soul, she embraced his passion, thinking little of the risks involved, captured in a whirlwind, driven by need, and fanned by love.

With whispered words spoken in Cherokee, he made love to her in every sense, coaxing her body once more to a dizzying, glorified state where she clawed at him for release.

When he complied, offering himself fully in return, the experience was beyond all the stories, all her dreams, all of her wishes.

Tears rolled down her cheeks, sliding past her ears. Her heart and her body were at one with this man.

"Sarah?" He braced on his elbows, his body still at one with hers. "I have hurt you. I am sorry, it was your first time and I should have been more careful."

She swallowed the tears blocking her throat and shook her head no.

"Then you are pleased?" He brushed her hair from her forehead, holding her gaze,

"Too much, I'm afraid." She turned from his concerned gaze, still warm from passion. And *this* is how it feels to have your heart break in two. To claim such happiness one moment and in the next realize you cannot have it for a lifetime.

"Sarah?" His voice brought her attention back to his face.

"I wish it could be different."

"Sarah." He sighed, dropping his forehead to hers and then rolled to his side tucking her in close, placing the other blanket over them. "Do not think of tomorrow, hold to what we have this night."

She nodded, feeling the warmth of his chest to her cheek.

The sounds of the night whispered around them as they held each other close.

"Sarah?" White Eagle lay on his back, looking at the stars.

"Yes?" She shifted so she could look, too, at the same sky.

"Come with me and I will show you how beautiful the river can be at night." He stood, holding out his hand.

"But I've seen—"

Naked and unashamed, he stared down at her and why she should feel such stirrings so soon after—

She reached for his hand. "Perhaps I've not seen everything."

He scooped her into his arms and carried her to the water, showing her in vivid detail everything he'd promised of its beauty.

∞

Sarah snuggled close to his magnificent slumbering body, her rebellious side weighing the possibilities of awakening him with the insatiable hunger he'd created in her.

She gazed through the trees, seeing the dawn of the morning sky brightening through the golden fall leaves. Here, they were far removed from the confusion and danger of the world. Their stolen moments were beyond the barriers of skin color and upbringing.

It wasn't that she had not thought of what her father would do should he discover she'd been with a man out of wedlock. Though she was unsure how much different his reaction would be to find that man was a Cherokee. Still she knew he would not be pleased with her wanton behavior

She'd made the decision. She'd never mention it. To the end of her days she would cherish this time as her own.

Sarah slid her palm over the hard plane of his broad chest, her body warming to the memory of his gentle touch urging her upward until her world exploded, making sense of what she felt for this man.

"We should be on our way."

His hand covered hers, stopping her meandering contemplation of his body.

"Please do not misunderstand my intentions. Surely, you do not think I would give myself to just any man?"

He turned his gaze to hers. "It is not in your nature, Sarah."

At least he understood that much, if nothing else. She hoped he adhered to a similar code.

"Sarah." He touched her cheek with the back of his hand. "I have never known someone like you. You have the spirit of a thousand horses and yet you are as sweet a breeze's whisper."

She stared at him, wondering what a lifetime of being cherished such as this would be like. "You have a poet's soul, sir." She smiled as she kissed the tip of his nose.

"I speak only the truth of what is inside me." He braced himself on his good elbow, pinning her with his dark gaze. "The truth is full of pain, Sarah. I cannot make you my wife, not now. Too much of the future of my people is uncertain and I cannot ask you to give up all you have known to follow that unknown path."

Bravery, a recently acquired attribute blossomed inside

her. "Then you will always be my husband. I shall not ever marry another if I cannot have you."

His smile, laced with sadness, did not quell the fire of passion in his eyes. "You will always have my heart, Sarah." He kissed her gently, lingering but a moment, and then pulled away when she circled her arms around his neck.

"It is time I took you to get Isabella. She will need a mother and a father. You are the only one who can help her."

That thought inspired yet another in her mind. "I could stay with you, White Eagle. Isabella and I could become your family—our family."

His gaze narrowed, searching her eyes and for a moment she thought he would agree. Her heart lifted in anticipation.

Hadn't he been the one to say that one cannot change the winds of fate? Perhaps this was her destiny, to live as his wife, and raise Isabella as their own, in the ways of peace. She could teach the Indian children of his clan the ways of the white man and help bridge the chasm between the two worlds.

"Is there not someone who will wonder where you are?"

Sarah smoothed her hands over his chest, relishing in the warm strength of his body close to hers. "Only my father and we have not been close since the death of my mother." She held his gaze. "I do not wish to leave you."

White Eagle smiled softly. "You are a brave woman, my Sarah, to offer such a sacrifice, but I cannot let you make it."

A cold shiver ran through Sarah's heart. Had she been

so naive to think her feelings would be reciprocated? Was the truth more than she cared to acknowledge?

"The things you spoke of last night. The feelings you said you had for me, were they untrue?" Sarah's stomach became queasy and she shoved against his chest, grabbing the blanket as she stood wrapping it around her. "You can't let me make this sacrifice, or *you won't?*" Her throat constricted with the tears threatening her composure.

"You speak in riddles. What I have inside for you does not matter in your white man's world. I doubt your father would be happy to find that I have known his daughter in this way."

"That is not my father's business, I am a grown woman."

"So you do not plan to tell him?"

Hoping for one last time to change his mind, she dropped to her knees. "We could live far from here. We could make our own life." Inside her heart pounded for an easy resolution, but none came.

"And you would not miss the life from which you came?" He stood, pulling on his breeches. "You have shown me, Sarah, that not all white men, or women, possess the same greed. I hope you will take with you the same thoughts of our time here."

He walked to the edge of the knoll, staring out at the river. "You should put on your clothes. I will find the coneflower and we will wrap your ankle."

She could say little more. It was painfully obvious that the moments they'd shared, while truly passionate at the time, were not much more than a whim of desire.

She dressed after he disappeared down the embankment, her emotions warring between her mind and her heart. In a scant few hours, she'd gone from young girl to a woman, and worse, she'd given this stranger her heart. Now she wondered if any man would have her for his wife. For that matter, if she could ever desire more, another man.

He returned shortly, holding a gray paste in his palm and a handful of berries in the other. "Here, we will find more as we travel. This will satisfy you for now."

White Eagle dropped the berries in her cupped hands then knelt before her. "Lift your skirt."

His methodic tone pierced her heart and she fought not to reach out to touch him. Her hand paused near his bent head, and instead tugged her skirt above her knee.

He worked quietly, spreading the salve over the wound, then with but a glance took his knife and sliced a swatch of her slip, tying it around her ankle.

"That will help heal the skin." He held the calf of her leg in his hand, inspecting his work.

"Your wound is healing well." She wanted him to remember the nights she'd cared for him, feeding him drops of sumac tea and placing fresh cool cloths to his fevered forehead. She wanted every moment to be burned into his memory, as hers would be for her.

He stood for a moment staring at her and without a word walked to his horse untying a small pouch from the reins.

He dropped to his knee in front of her and dug into the pouch, keeping his gaze fixed on her. Pulling the necklace into view, he leaned forward carefully tying it around her neck. "It was my mother's. Given to her on her wedding day by my father. He made it for her."

Sarah turned the delicately fashioned piece of pure

gold in her fingers. The detail of the design bringing to mind the exquisite love and care the designer possessed. "It looks like a bird." She inspected it closer; even the feathers were hewn properly.

"It is a cardinal. Cherokee believe she is the daughter of the sun."

The huskiness in his voice clearly indicated what the necklace meant to him.

Her gaze traveled to his. "Why do you give this to me?" She searched his face hoping he had changed his mind. Perhaps he would ask her to stay.

White Eagle brushed the back of his hand over her cheek. Love blatantly shone in the depth of his gaze. "I do not wish you to think I will not remember you, Sarah. Every time the *svnoyi ehi nvdo* is a full in the night sky, every time I drink from the soothing waters of a *Uweyu*, every time the *Nvdo iga ehi* breaks new on the morning horizon, I *will* remember."

He kissed her gently and she held his face, as her tears pressed against his cheeks.

CHAPTER SIXTEEN

The Encounter

"It appears, my brother, that your wound has healed."

Tsula's voice broke White Eagle's hold on Sarah. He whirled standing protectively in front of her.

"Does she satisfy as well as a woman of your own blood, White Eagle?" Still astride his great horse, Tsula circled around until he stood facing them again.

White Eagle's gaze darted to the nearby woods searching for the rest of the renegade followers.

"It is only you and I—" Tsula dismounted, studying Sarah with a narrow gaze. "And the woman." He paused as though assessing Sarah's worth. "Though she is thin, she would offer warmth on a cold night."

His jaw clenched at the manner in which he spoke of her, but White Eagle held his anger at bay, knowing that Tsula was sparring for a fight. He kept silent as he searched for a way out of this predicament without bloodshed.

White Eagle reached behind, pulling Sarah to her feet and away from the appraising eye of the friend who'd now become his enemy. "I am taking her to the white man's camp," he stated.

His friend's deep laughter echoed through the forest. "And do you think they will allow you to live once they have you?" the warrior shouted in anger.

"Better to take my chances with a stranger's face, than with one who masks as a friend." White Eagle nudged

Sarah back, taking a few steps to put greater distance between them. He needed to get Sarah close to his horse. Perhaps she could escape while he detained Tsula.

"Why do you risk your life for this woman? Who is this that has ensnared you so boldly?" The glint in his eye spoke loudly that the man knew more than he revealed.

Before he could speak, Sarah stepped from behind and placed her hands squarely on her hips in blatant confrontation. "I am Sarah Reynolds, daughter of Charles William Reynolds. He happens to be a very important man at the camp."

White Eagle's heart went cold. He turned to meet Sarah's defiant look, and the shock on his face, caused her expression to turn to bewilderment.

My Sarah is the daughter of the man who murdered my father?

There was after a short silence, then a dreadful calm in Tsula's voice, "Yes, I am well acquainted with *who* your father is, Sarah Reynolds."

Nausea rose in his throat as White Eagles gaze spun back to his one-time friend.

The tug of a cynical smile played at the corner of his mouth. "I see this comes as a surprise to you, my friend. Fate plays odd tricks, does it not?"

Sarah's hands dropped weak at her sides, her gaze fixed on his.

White Eagle's world tipped askew as the past collided with the future. His heart ached with the knowledge of fates trickery, almost as if mocking him.

The horrid memory of that night three years ago came rushing back to White Eagle. Upon returning home one evening from a tribunal council, he and his father had encountered a masked group of white riders. When things got out of hand, a lone bullet snuffed out the life of his father. He was never sure who fired the shot, but he remembered the warning he received from the man on his horse staring down at him as he held his dying father.

"You would do well to leave now. There is nothing here for your people any longer. Your day is past. It is time for progress. Mark the words of Charles Reynolds, boy." And with that he rode off into the dark night.

He'd wanted to go after the men, his anger blazing red as a flame, but his father made him vow to stay. He became a man that night. His father had made him the head of the family, protector, and provider—as he lay dying in his arms.

Now, in the form of a woman more beautiful than any dream, his nightmare, Charles Reynolds had reappeared. Once again, inflicting excruciating pain to his heart.

He staggered briefly as he pushed Sarah behind him, backing her to a tree to protect her. Though his insides churned at the image of her father's complacent face as he rode away, he fought hard to believe that his daughter was anything like him.

Not *his* Sarah. Not the woman whom he'd just given his heart to.

"Perhaps the gods have given you this opportunity to make things right?" Tsula reached for the rifle encased in a sling over his back. "To balance the injustice of loss of life as Cherokee code dictates."

Despite what White Eagle believed of the way his people had lived for many years, life had also been a cruel teacher. He believed now a man must take responsibility for his own sin. No longer could the innocent suffer for the atonement of the guilty.

"She is innocent." White Eagle kept one arm across Sarah as he held Tsula's hardened gaze. Where had their lives divided? When did this blood brother become someone not to trust?

He shrugged. "Perhaps there is better use in her alive."

"What is he talking about?" Sarah whispered fiercely.

"She does not know her father's reputation?" Tsula tapped the rifle to his palm.

White Eagle eyed his old friend and remembered the hunting knife strapped to his leg. "She knows nothing. She is innocent."

The warrior gave a short laugh and raised his brow. "Well, not entirely it would seem, given what I came upon." He took a leisurely step toward them. "Perhaps though, she would make a bargaining tool."

"What does he—?" She gave him a questioning expression.

White Eagle interrupted her with a fierce look of warning as he moved his body in front of her keeping an eye to Tsula, quietly seeking to gain better access to Sarah.

"You cannot fight with one arm, my friend." He took another step and White Eagle poised to attack.

"Perhaps you should ask your scout?" White Eagle knew he was buying time. Soon Tsula would tire of the banter and lash out blindly. There was a chance Sarah could escape then in the confusion.

The warrior's jaw twitched from the strain of his clenched teeth. "He was a good man, a brave warrior. He fought well and he died well."

"He was a worthy opponent." White Eagle agreed. The two stared at each other in silence as if weighing what the other would do next.

"Let us be reasonable. I give you my word. No harm shall come to her. I will use her only to find reason with her father." He pointed the butt of his rifle towards him. "You can deal with justice in the way you wish."

"What makes you think that you can use people like they were animals to barter with? I refuse to be a part of it. My father is an intelligent man; he would gladly sit down and speak with you."

"Sarah, I must ask your silence." White Eagle spoke gently, his gaze trained on Tsula's piercing look.

Tsula's sudden raucous laughter brought White Eagle upright, his body tense with anticipation of his next move. "This one is full of spirit, White Eagle. I can see why you wish to keep her for yourself."

"I do not have claim to her." White Eagle spoke the words, though even as he spoke in his heart the words were a lie. She would always be his.

"And what manner of passion did I stumble on, White Eagle?" Tsula taunted.

"I will not let you take her. This is not the way." He could feel Sarah's breath on his shoulder as she listened closely from behind.

The brilliant rays of dawn began to peek through the morning mist, streaking the forest with beams of filtered light. The challenge was growing more intense and White Eagle sensed it in every fiber of his being. This confrontation was not going to end peacefully.

"What you think is wrong or right is of no concern to me, White Eagle. If you will not give her to me freely, then I will be forced to take her from you." His voice grew louder as he positioned his rifle, lowering his aim at White Eagle's chest.

Hoping he would take the challenge offered White Eagle belittled the use of Tsula's rifle in hope for a hand-to-hand battle. At least then he might have a chance and so might Sarah. "Traditional challenges have always warranted a warrior to use his wit and his hands."

With a growl of a laugh, Tsula tossed the gun to the ground and lunged for White Eagle. "So it will be."

He shoved Sarah away from him as pain, sharp and swift raced like lightning through his arm. He knew Tsula would go for his injured arm first, to gain his advantage.

White Eagle dropped to the ground, rolling from Tsula, catching only a glimpse of Sarah as she searched the grass he hoped for the rifle.

He leapt to his feet facing his familiar opponent, giving him little time to stand upright before barreling headfirst into his stomach. Satisfied with the muffled groan forced from the warrior's mouth White Eagle toppled over his opponent, only to feel the hard grasp of a hand around his ankle.

He flopped to his back staring up at the face of untamed determination that could well cost him his life.

"You would do well to give her to me, White Eagle. I give you my word—"

"Your word means little." He bent his leg, planting his foot firmly in Tsula's belly and hurled him over his head.

In a blur of blue skirts, Sarah rushed forward holding a large rock above her head.

"Sarah, no!" His words fell on deaf ears as she reared her body back and sent the rock hurling towards Tsula's head.

White Eagle's breath caught in his throat as he watched her stumble backward and fall.

In one swift motion, Tsula rolled from the path of the rock and White Eagle felt the tug on his leg. Before he could react, Tsula had leapt to his feet and pulled Sarah up against him. The rock bounced inches from White Eagle's head.

His sickened gaze returned to the pair. His heart seared with pain in seeing his hunting knife poised at Sarah's throat. White Eagle pushed himself to his feet, shaking not from the trauma inflicted to his bleeding shoulder, but from the look in Sarah's fear-stricken eyes.

He was losing blood quickly, causing their duel image to swim hazily before him. "No harm to her—" his breath came hard, "you will answer to me."

"You are hardly in the position to give orders, my friend." He shifted Sarah's head, stretching for full view, his blade against her alabaster throat.

"Do not be a fool Tsula." White Eagle reached for them, shaking his head, but a wave of nausea dropped him to his knees.

"Still, I can use her better alive, than dead."

"This way is no better than Reynolds and his people." He lifted his face to Tsula, glancing at Sarah.

Her gaze flashed to his. It was obvious she did not realize the terror her father and his men had inflicted on the Cherokee people or his family.

"I am sorry, Sarah." He grabbed his shoulder feeling the stickiness of his own blood oozing between his fingers. There was nothing more he could do for now. Surely Tsula would take her to his camp and there create a plan with his men to contact Charles Reynolds and bargain with him for his daughter's life. He needed to get to Running Doe in the meantime, knowing he needed help to stop Tsula.

"What will you do with her?" White Eagle challenged the Indian's honor. "You are betrothed to my sister, or have you forgotten?"

Tsula lifted Sarah astride his horse, swinging up behind her, he held her with one powerful arm preventing her escape. "Running Doe has left with the other members of those who have chosen to escape migration by hiding in the mountains. A fact I am sure you are well aware of." He twisted as the impatient steed fought the reins. "I belong to no one except for the good of the Cherokee people. I cannot cloud the purpose of my mission with desires of the flesh. Our pact is broken."

"Your word, Tsula, as a Cherokee," White Eagle warned, struggling to his feet again, "I will find you if one hair on her head is harmed." He blinked, holding the warriors gaze as long as he could.

Tsula raised a brow as he glanced over his shoulder, then dug his heels into the horse's side and rode off at a dead run.

White Eagle held Sarah's gaze, his body racked with the pain engulfing his re-injured shoulder, but his heart ached with much greater pain. He stumbled to his horse and hope he would live long enough to get to Running Doe and his people.

"I want that savage found!" The angry man slammed his fist to the table toppling over the glass of his favorite whiskey, splattering his recent reports.

"I need only to follow Tsula and his men. I am certain to discover White Eagle's whereabouts."

"I don't care if you have to search every injun hut from here to Arkansas—" The man coughed, sputtering as his face purpled in familiar rage.

The Cherokee messenger sensed now the desperation in the man's eyes. Perhaps it was a good time to ask for what he required in return. "Mr. Reynolds, sir. In order to bring this man, White Eagle to you, I would require something to assure the danger involved would be worth the risk."

Silence hung heavy in the one room cabin used as the headquarters for Charles Reynolds for the better part of the last five years. He'd given his time here originally in hopes of establishing a future for him and Sarah. The private New York school cost him dearly and when the opportunity to be hired by the government was presented it was his way out. Recently, however, the reins had been pulled in tighter and the suggestions made in the form of demand became more stringent to the governments desperation to their cause. Not a day went by but what Charles Reynolds could hear the high-pitched shrill voice of his dead wife reminding him of his failure as a provider to his family.

He cleared his throat, establishing his composure, and then carefully picked up his glass and set it upright. "Have you been compensated fairly for your work in the past?'

The Indian squirmed in the chair; sweat broke out on his upper lip. He nodded.

"Then there is no reason to think this time will be any different." Reynolds stepped from behind the desk, straightening his vest as he glanced at the ceiling in thought. He stopped behind the man, tamping down the anger seething inside him. He needed this man to find Sarah. Once this task was complete, he would gladly deliver this man exactly what he deserved.

"Perhaps there is a way to avoid migration for you and your family? Would that be an adequate incentive for this task?" Reynolds clasped his hands behind his back.

The messenger sat stoically, staring straight ahead. "That would be most generous of you, sir," he replied.

Reynolds smiled. The Cherokee were so easily persuaded with honesty. "Fine. Go now and bring White Eagle to me."

"Yes, sir." The messenger did not let his gaze leave the floor as he left the cabin.

Reynolds grasped the rungs of the chair, staring at its now empty seat. Did White Eagle know whom it was he held prisoner? His stomach grew nauseous at the thought of the possible savagery that could be inflicted on his daughter. If she was harmed in any way, he would see to it himself that the remaining Cherokee nation would pay—and White Eagle would be the example.

In blind rage he lifted the chair, flinging it across the room.

Sarah shivered, fearful of what might have happened to White Eagle. Fearful too, of finding out more about the mystery surrounding her father and the allegations that were being made against him.

She pulled the blanket tighter around her as she huddled near the inside wall of the empty hut they'd put her in. Tsula had not harmed her, though his manner had been gruff, he'd simply given orders upon their arrival at what appeared to be deserted village to have her placed in the hut and the door guarded. Obviously, he anticipated that someone might come for her.

Sarah swallowed against the dryness in her throat. She'd not eaten all morning and she was thirsty. Her stomach protested as much as she glanced at her stark surroundings. The white adobe-like walls might have surrounded a peaceful family at one time. A few baskets and pieces of pottery lay clumped together in the middle of the room, as though planned for travel then left at the last minute.

She glanced down at the blue blanket she sat on and her eyes stung remembering White Eagle's explanation of the wedding ceremony. What would happen to her? Would her fate be the same as Laura and Mr. Bixby? Her stomach lurched at the possibility and she pressed her back to the cool stone of the wall trying to gain her composure. She would need every bit of her sense if she were going to think of a way out of this situation.

Outside she heard deep voices, some of them angry, most speaking in tones too low for her to clearly hear what was being said. She strained to hear some of the discussion.

"Already they are forcing our people from the land. I have heard of many who are waiting in stockades as though they are in prisons."

"Their great chief ignores what his council advises."

Sarah knew there was debate in the legislature regarding the markings of territories. Yet, she'd also heard stories of compliance between Cherokee and the white settlers. More disturbing, she realized those particular snippets of news had come from the letters her father had sent.

Her ears piqued to her captor's voice, "We will send a few men ahead to advise the camp we have the woman,

Sarah Reynolds. We will demand in writing that all raids cease at once and that the white settlers will not intrude on the land of our fathers."

"Will they listen, Tsula?"

Sarah could see the flaw in Tsula's simple plan and she suspected it would not work. In all likelihood, those sent would fall before they had the opportunity to speak. Then what would become of her?

Perhaps if she spoke to Tsula, persuaded him to take her with him to the camp, her father would be more willing to compromise. Surely her father would listen if she were to act as mediator. There was more discussion, though their voices lowered further preventing her from hearing Tsula's answer

"You have fed the woman?" Tsula's voice nearby suddenly inquired of the guard outside the door. Sarah straightened, waiting for his entrance. She lifted the piece of fried bread left in her bowl, stuffing bits quickly in her mouth in case they would take the remaining food from her. She might sit for days without food, but right now she thirsted for water.

"Excuse me?" She lifted her voice, hoping to get the guard's attention. Perhaps Tsula was still outside.

The curtain over the entrance swept aside and a fierce looking man covered only with a loincloth, entered the room. His rugged face all but snarled at her query.

Sarah eyed the spear crooked in the Indians elbow. "Would it be possible to get something to drink?" She knew from her eavesdropping that he spoke a little English. Keeping her chin high, she held the warrior's gaze hoping to show she would not be intimidated. Still she wondered it wise whether to ask to speak to his leader.

Before she could consider it however, the man left, grumbling under his breath and returned within moments with a pottery jug.

He slammed the container into her hands, splashing the contents over its sides and down Sarah's outstretched arms. Determined to prove that not all white people were as ruthless as these few thought, she forced a pleasant smile. "Thank you."

His piercing, black eyes, indicative of his lineage, stared coldly at her, and then he turned on his heel and left her alone.

Relieved for the water to quench her thirst, she wiped her mouth and sighed. Whether from nerves or exhausted from a night of passion, Sarah could not determine the reason for her sudden tiredness. Her gaze rose to the hole in the ceiling seeing the blue skies above, and yet in the shadows of the hut, she shivered from a chill. Resigned that she would have to wait for the opportunity to speak to Tsula, she lay down and thought about White Eagle, wondering if he would he attempt to rescue her? Hugging the blanket around her, she drifted into a dreamless sleep.

More than a few days passed as she drifted in and out of a delirious sleep. At first she thought maybe they'd given her some type of herb to drug her abilities, but she realized that she'd eaten precious little, nor had she had much to drink since her arrival. Each day she grew more concerned that perhaps White Eagle had decided their parting was for the best. After all, the vows they'd taken that night were only a mock ceremony.

Sarah choked back the sensation of tears, though no

wetness reached her eyes. Closing her eyes to her fatigue and her probable fate, she slept.

A small thump woke Sarah and as her eyes adjusted to the darkness around her she realized she was not alone in the room.

"Who is it? Who's there?" She rose, backing against the wall, blinking away the fatigue still clouding her mind.

The shadowy figure crept close to the ground silently making its way to Sarah.

She held her breath, her mind conjuring all manner of horrid endings.

"It is Running Doe. Do not be afraid, "she whispered.

A small hand touched the covering on Sarah's arm and she jerked in response.

"White Eagle has sent me." She leaned close, so close Sarah could feel the heat of her breath.

Fear and panic clawed at her throat as she attempted to speak, the desert dryness making matters worse. "Is he all right? His shoulder? Where is he?" Sarah grasped the young girl's shoulders holding tight.

"He is well." Running Does covered Sarah's hands and pried them from her shoulders. "He wanted me to come in his place, to speak with you. He says I am like a mouse."

Sarah's eyes welled. "Then he is well?"

Running Doe nodded. "Much blood was lost, but he rests now with his people. The medicine woman is watching over him. The tribe offers much prayer." Her gaze darted to the door, then to the hole in the roof. "I cannot stay. I was sent to tell you that White Eagle will come for you at daybreak."

"How—? It is far too dangerous—"

The Indian woman silenced Sarah by placing a finger

to her lips. "My brother is stubborn, even more when it comes to matters of the heart."

Sarah's heart warmed with hope for the first time in many hours. The flesh of her cheeks heated with shy pleasure.

Running Doe tipped her head as though studying her. "I sense it is the same for you, Sarah." her hand brushed across Sarah's belly resting but for a moment, "as it shall be for your children."

She turned then, and crouching low crept back to the rope hanging from the hole in the ceiling.

Sarah watched her shimmy up the rope quietly and disappeared through the thatched roof. Her mind, not yet fully grasping Running Doe's words, lay in a state of shock. She lowered herself to the floor, staring up at the black sky and the stars twinkling beyond, until she could no longer keep her lids open.

In her dreams that night, she sat in a meadow watching a young girl with bouncing blonde tendrils run through tall green grass, collecting wildflowers. Her laughter touched a secret part of Sarah and caused the toddler on her lap to giggle with delighted glee as he clapped his pudgy hands.

Sarah gazed down with love at how the summer breeze blew the little boy's black tuft of hair straight up as though reaching for the summer sun. Bittersweet memories played in her heart as she gazed at the boy, a small replica of his father.

The young girl showed her the ring of flowers she made and Sarah smiled her approval, nodding as the girl's smile lit up her face. She turned and lovingly placed the wreath over the crude cross marking the simple grave.

CHAPTER SEVENTEEN

Common Ground

Nausea rose in Sarah's throat and her body dripped from waves of heat and then cold racking her body.

"It is soon time to go to your father. Wake now, he will wish to see that you are well. Eat what we have brought for you." Tsula showed no regard for the way she appeared.

Her hair clung to her cheek and neck and she could smell the scent of her own perspiration. Somehow overnight she'd developed an illness, perhaps from tainted water? Sarah struggled to open her eyelids, heavy with fatigue. The heavy aroma of smoked meat suddenly wafted under her nose, and the bile erupted, bolting her body upright.

Before she could cover her mouth, she'd vomited the meager contents of her stomach, catching the horrified expression on Tsula's face as landed squarely to his chest.

His eyes widened in disgust.

"I'm sorry—" her words slurred in her lethargic state. All she wanted, what was more important than life itself, was to ease the nausea with sleep.

"Have you carried this sickness for long?"

She feebly shook her head no, shutting her eyes to the daylight peeking in past the blanket.

Tsula grunted as he batted the slimy residue from his chest. "There are few reasons to cause a woman to behave in such a manner." He glanced at her with curiosity.

"White Eagle's actions are not apparently as pure as his words."

Sarah shook her head. "No, it wasn't like that." She took a deep breath hoping to calm the next rumbling of her stomach. "I—I love him." There she'd said it, not to White Eagle, but to his tribesman—the one man according to White Eagle who knew him best, or had at one time.

Tsula's hand froze in mid-air as he stared at her. "It is not permitted."

She wanted to argue, to tell him that they had already made their marital vows and there was nothing he could do to stop them. Instead, between the nausea and the truth if its origin, Sarah cared little what rules Tsula was governed by. "It seems that you cannot stop fate." A wry smile formed on her lips. "White Eagle taught me that."

"He will try to come for you," he barked, the words in frustration, implying yet another dilemma he would be forced to deal with.

Yet in his tone, Sarah heard softness—perhaps the conscience of an old friend, perhaps nothing more than a respect for life—at least the life inside her that was—in part—Cherokee.

With a heavy sigh Tsula sat on the ground, folding his legs as though in meeting with the great tribal chief. As if weighing his options, he studied her until Sarah thought she would go mad. Then without warning, he stood. "Come, we will go together to see your father. Perhaps this news will add credence to our requests." He reached down, grabbed her arm, and pulled her to her feet.

Dizziness swept over her as she wobbled on watery legs. "You've killed more than a dozen innocent people.

Only Isabella and I survived, and only because of White Eagle."

He paused, his grip still clamped to her arm. "*You* will make him see that what happened was not meant to end in such a way. It was meant to frighten in the same way as the white man has frightened our people."

Confusion reigned supreme in Sarah's mind as once again allegations were set upon people associated with her father. "What is this nonsense you speak of?" She waved her hand, and then clamped it over her mouth. Images, some hazy, others clear danced in her head. "I must sit down for a moment."

She slumped to the ground, leaving Tsula holding the blanket she'd been wrapped in.

"We have sources that tell us it is your father who leads the terror raids on our people late at night." Tsula dropped the blanket at her feet and paced the hut as he spoke, "The white man does not like that we have our own schools, our own language, even our own alphabet. They despise our governing council and have taken by force much of the land and its gold that my people have prospered from for many generations."

He turned to Sarah, piercing her with a gaze that directed all his anger of the white settler to her. "No longer are they content to share the riches of the land with the Cherokee. They are greedy and crave more. They want us to leave the home of our fathers and their father's before them."

Though Sarah did not want to hear of such atrocities, she listened as Tsula gave specific accounts of women and children being terrorized by men too cowardly to reveal their faces, hiding them by the same black scarves that had become their calling card.

Her heart ached for the plight of White Eagle's people and because she knew how far the determination of Tsula, no matter how misguided, was willing to go to fight for their beliefs.

"Let me talk to my father." Sarah reached for Tsula's hand. "Help me, and I will help you." She waited, hoping her plea would not fall on deaf ears.

He stepped forward, grasping her hand and pulled her to her feet once again. "Let us go visit the medicine woman. She will know what to do for your illness." He paused then assessing her from head to toe. "Your father would not be pleased to think we had not taken care of you. You may bathe in the river and we will make tolerable your illness."

Sarah stepped from the hut into the early light of dawn, squinting as her eyes focused from the shadows. The fierce man who'd been her guard turned, an open frown plastered to his face. Sarah followed his gaze to Tsula's chest.

"I am taking the woman to the river to bathe. Prepare the men to go to camp."

The man raised his brow and gave a quick nod.

"There is privacy near a grove of trees, you can bathe there." Tsula stared straight ahead, his tone authoritative and grim.

"I am sorry." Sarah carefully walked behind the powerful man, watching her footing over the branches strewn in the path.

The early sounds of birds twittered in the trees high above.

"Water will wash everything away, "he replied keeping

his gaze ahead.

"Perhaps not everything." She jerked to a stop to prevent running into his formidable back.

"There are some things that will not as easily be cleansed," He turned, his gaze intense and yet not without a trace of compassion. "Perhaps I was blind not to see that there is good blood that flows in some white people."

Her eyes welled at his admission.

∞

"You are certain she is unharmed." White Eagle impatiently waited as his sister redressed his wound.

For many days he'd lay half-conscious fearful of what Tsula planned for Sarah. He'd mentally chastised himself for allowing his passion for her to get out of control. Yet he might just as well try to stop the raging river's strong current. He had no regret for what happened between them, other than the possibility his seed might place her in greater danger with her father. The dawn of this possibility came crashing into his thoughts and the image of Sarah, her belly, round with his child, blazed in his mind.

"You are fortunate to have the use of your arm, my brother." She glanced up, casting him a tolerant look as she tightened the last knot of his sling.

"Why is it that you dance around my question?" He lifted her chin with his hand, searching her eyes for an answer.

"She is as well as can be expected—" she kept her focus to inspecting her work, and then grinned at him—"for a white woman."

He dropped his hand, checked his sling, and glanced up to find her smiling. It was hard to stay angry with her for very long. It had always been that way between them. Teasing each other, but defending one another, to the death if need be.

"You will see for yourself soon enough, my brother." His sister shrugged and then turned back to the task of rolling the extra strips of cloth used as dressings his wound.

Frustrated by her evasiveness, but more anxious to get to Sarah, he slid his quiver of arrows over his good shoulder.

"How many men will you take with you?" Running Doe continued to roll the bandage strips, placing them in a basket for storage.

"I will go alone. I cannot risk any more lives."

"You would be wise to not risk your own life so freely." She didn't look up, but kept busy cleaning up the medicinal supplies.

"What I choose to do, I do for the good of all."

"*This* sounds much like another stubborn warrior we both know."

"This is not a time to quarrel, my sister." White Eagle sighed. He headed toward the door.

Running Doe leapt to her feet blocking his way. "And tell me great warrior, how do you plan to hold a bow and arrow?" She planted herself in front of him, her hands firm upon her slim hips.

"With the blessing of the Great Spirit, I will have no need of them." He spotted Sarah's satchel laying on the floor and bent to retrieve it. He held it, remembering the moment he chose to look through her journal, wanting to find a way to be near her. It was then he discovered the drawing she'd done of him while he'd slept. To see himself in such detail through her eyes and know that she planned to keep them with her forever, both humbled and excited him.

It was yet another affirmation of her feelings, confirming those he'd tried to hide deep in his heart. Perhaps her idea of learning to live with his clan was not such an impossible notion.

"Be wise, my brother and have someone waiting in the woods." Running Doe caught his good arm as he walked by.

"It will be well, do not worry." He placed his hand on her shoulder and kissed her forehead. Hoping for the grace of the Great Spirit and for protection, he took a deep breath and smiled at his sister in confidence. "Do this while I am away. Gather the women and make plans for a traditional marriage ceremony."

Running Doe's face lit with a bright smile. "And who, may I ask; would I be preparing the ceremonial fire for?"

"With any hope, I will convince your willful intended to settle down to a quiet family life."

"And what of my willful brother?" she called after him.

He grinned over his shoulder seeing her soft smile. The image stayed clearly etched in his mind as he rode toward Tsula's camp.

CHAPTER EIGHTEEN

Anguished Cry

White Eagle peered through the heavy mist blanketing the valley. Brushing the heavy dew from his eyelids he squinted, trying to discern where the meadow ended and the forest began.

The valley, this morning lay deathly quiet in an unusual silent shroud. Every sense he possessed as a hunter heightened in strength as his horse plodded through the tall grass.

He knew that through the forest to the west was the first of the Cherokee camps, now most likely abandoned by its residents. Using logic, this would be the best place for Tsula to have his men and hence, Sarah. The white man's fort was but a short distance over a low ridge of hills to the east, near a fork in the river.

A fearful premonition skated at the edge of his spirit, making him uneasy. His horse snorted as though he too sensed something was not quite right.

He prodded the horse forward, keeping his sharp gaze searching ahead. The only sound was the pampas grass brushing against the horse's side and the heavy breathing of the animal.

The horse stopped in his tracks, and at the same moment the hairs on the back of White Eagle's neck stood on edge. His gaze snapped behind him to a flash of brown coming toward him at lightning speed.

He drew his bow; his teeth clenched fighting the pain shooting through his shoulder, not waiting for the misty apparition to come into full view.

Sweat broke out on his upper lip as he waited for a better view, hoping his arm would hold out long enough to find good aim.

"White Eagle!" Running Doe's urgent voice issued through the foggy haze.

Frustration quickly replaced relief as his sister, on her buckskin pony came into view. He dropped his bow and turned, his ears piqued to yet another sound that struck fear into his heart.

"No!" His horrified gaze followed the familiar sound as it streaked through the mist narrowly missing his arm, instead finding its resting place in the middle of Running Doe's chest.

The impact of the deadly arrow knocked her off the back of her horse and his heart froze as he watched her body fall with a dull thud to the cold ground.

He jerked as though waking from a terrible nightmare, and blinked trying to erase the sight of his sister's face staring up at him.

She reached for him, her expression full of sorrow, tinged with fear.

White Eagle leapt from his horse, searching the horizon quickly before he knelt at her side to see what damage the arrow had rendered.

He cradled her in his lap, searching her eyes, wanting to ease her pain, but to pull the arrow from its mark would surely cause greater damage. All he could do was hold her in his arms and think of his father. His heart cried out in anguish that he'd not been able to fulfill his duty to protect her as his father wished.

Tears welled in his eyes, as a greater storm brewed within him. "Tsula intends to take Sarah himself to the camp. I was afraid they would try to stop you—" She coughed, and blood splattered on the hand she clung to. Her words, broken, came with great effort, "There is more you should know—" Running Doe's eyes widened as her hand grappled for her brother's arm. "Sarah—"

Her breathing stopped and White Eagle shook her. "Do not die my little mouse. Do not leave me this way. Not now."

She gasped and it brought up a trickle of blood, her eyes fluttered open, but only briefly. She smiled, though weak, flooded his heart with hope. "It is well." She patted his hand, smearing her blood on his skin. "Our father waits for me. I hear my name being called." Her gaze flickered to his. "You will know what it is like to be a father." And with that her soul was set free. Her body fell limp in his arms.

White Eagle's mind could not comprehend all that had happened. He could only stare at his sister's lifeless body and wonder what great evil would take the life of someone so good and pure. Like a wounded animal, he moaned his loss as he embraced her against him. No white man could have such precision aim, which meant whomever did this foul deed was one of his own people.

Placing her bloodied palm over his heart, he lifted his face to the ominous, gray sky. His anguished cry broke the ethereal silence.

Sarah rode in silence, encircled from all sides by Tsula's

men. The brewed concoction the medicine women gave her eased the nausea, but fatigue still plagued her.

Running Doe's words re-played in her mind. "He will come for you at dawn's light."

Sarah lifted her gaze to her surroundings, but was unable to get beyond the hard, stoic expressions of the warriors riding close beside her.

Tsula raised his hand and in the same instant the entire group stopped. A distant sound like that of a dying animal echoed in the morning mist.

Her heart twisted at the animal's possible pain, its torment sounding eerily human.

The messenger rode hard through the morning mist, away from the primal scream of the warrior left behind. The arrow intended for White Eagle had missed and struck another, riding behind him. Fear struck in his heart that perhaps it was the daughter of Charles Reynolds. In any event, it was not wise to wait to find out, so he'd turned on his heel, running fast through the mist-sodden grass, and found his way back to his horse.

His mind searched what his next step should be, though his options were painfully limited. He could not go back to the camp until he knew for sure who White Eagle's companion was. Yet, he could not go back to the site knowing White Eagle still lived. Was it possible White Eagle was thinking of taking her to the fort himself?

The man brought up the reins to his horse nearly toppling them both over backwards.

"I see you are in haste, my friend. Where are you heading?" Ahead, blocking his path, Tsula sat astride his great horse, flanked by his warriors on all sides. Behind him rode a white woman, her expression pasty with illness. She wore a blanket draped around her shoulders.

The man breathed a sigh of relief. *Surely this was Sarah Reynolds.* His fear of Charles Reynolds wrath faded, though not his concerns over White Eagle's haunting scream. Still, he could make the best of the present circumstances. After all isn't this what he did best?

"I am glad to see you again, my friend." He peered around Tsula in an attempt to gain better view. "Is this the white woman lost from the wagon train?" His black derby, a recently acquired gift, slid and he reached up to prevent it from toppling off.

Seven arrows suddenly pointed at his chest.

The man swallowed, slowly straightening upright. Carefully his gaze found Tsula's. "Your men seem on edge, great warrior."

"And you look as though you have seen a ghost." Tsula tipped his head studying the man.

The man attempted a chuckle that died in his throat. "It is a fine morning for a ride." He eyed the Indians as he spoke, his heart beginning to pound as his spirit sensed that something was not quite right.

"What is your interest in the woman?" Tsula held up his hand and the weapons lowered, but only to the laps of the tribesmen.

The messenger shrugged. "It is of no concern to me personally. I know that Mr. Reynolds will be pleased to see she is well. This gesture of goodwill could work well for you and your men, Tsula." He brushed the brim of his hat in confidence. "With my help, of course."

A moment of silence clicked by. Sarah's skin shivered from the tension in the air, yet she could not discern its origin. Who was this man, with the coloring of a Cherokee and the clothing of a well-to-do white man?

Tsula shifted, sitting taller to give greater advantage of his enormous build. "Perhaps you've been sent as a scout to detain us until Reynolds and his men can ready for our arrival?"

The man's smile dropped from his expression and he swallowed, noticeably nervous as his eyes darted to the tribesmen.

"No, I have only been out for a morning ride." His words squeezed through a catch in his throat, which he tried to cover with a cough.

"Were you also hunting?"

The man's face noticeably paled in color.

Sarah knew that Tsula was referring to the animal's cries. With the noble reverence the Cherokee had for hunting, an animal left wounded was considered taboo to the Great Spirit.

He shook his head, and shrugged. "I have not...been hunting this day." Sweat broke out on the man's face and he smiled as he tugged at the collar of his pristine white shirt.

Tsula held the man's gaze as one or two of the tribesmen around them shifted nervously on their horses.

Sarah pressed close to Tsula's back, fearful now there was going to be a confrontation and this man was not going to live.

She started to speak, but held her tongue when Tsula spoke.

"Perhaps you will do us the honor of riding ahead and let Reynolds know, that his daughter is well, and that we come in peace, to talk with him."

The man pondered his request, and then nodded slowly. "Perhaps you are wise great warrior. I will go ahead and prepare for your arrival." He puffed out his chest with pride. "I will speak to Reynolds myself and convince him that you come in peace." The man lifted his reins and tugged them to the left, carefully prodding his horse through the path opened for his passage by Tsula's men.

Sarah caught his quick glance as he rode by and something in his eyes sent a chill though her.

He rode away from the group in silence, and then without looking back, nudged his horse to pick up its pace.

Tsula and his men quietly held their gaze on the messenger as he rode ahead, soon lost in the curve in the trail through the trees. Shortly thereafter, Tsula pointed to one of the fierce-looking men of his party, and with but a nod, instructed the man to follow the messenger.

Without hesitation, the Indian dug his heels into the horse's sides and rode after the man.

With a brief backward glance, Tsula motioned forward and the entourage continued slowly along the path at an unhurried pace.

Sarah tried to push from her mind the fears lodged there like a bullet—afraid of what might happen and yet hoping for a miracle. She bowed her head and whispered a silent prayer that White Eagle would not try any heroics to rescue her against these men. Their mission was intent and no one would dare stop them now without facing certain death.

The muffled sound of one of the horse's rough snorts broke her from her reverie. She looked up and her heart stopped. She covered her mouth to prevent the scream clawing its way up her throat at the sight of the messenger lifeless on the ground. She shut her eyes against the vacant look on the dead man's face, the fear, still fresh, his neck slit with hunter's precision from ear-to-ear. It could not have been more than a few minutes since Tsula's rider galloped after the well-dressed man.

The rider summoned for the gruesome task climbed onto his horse, wiping the blade of his knife on his breeches.

Shaking, she held onto Tsula for fear she would fall when she fainted. Bile climbed in her throat as she clung tight to his sides, her body began to shake uncontrollably.

"He was not true to his people." He spoke loud so she could hear what he had to say. As though this knowledge would justify his order. "He lived to profit from his lies."

Sarah pressed her forehead against the flesh of Tsula's back. *What was happening to her? What was happening to the world?* She wanted to be back at school apart from this senseless bloodshed, but in doing so, meant giving up any chance of seeing White Eagle again.

"I am sorry you had to see this," Tsula spoke over his shoulder, "but I am not sorry he is dead." He straightened as though brushing Sarah's tears from his skin.

She hung her head and let the tears flow freely, but she did not look back.

With what seemed only minutes they came upon a clearing. Ahead she heard the commanding soldier barking out orders during morning inspection. Captain McKenna's handsome face popped into her mind and she thought of his smile and his gracious manner, his straight-shouldered stance as he led the wagon train. Tears fell, as one face after another appeared in her memory—Mr. Bixby, Laura, and then little Isabella. A strange foreboding clamped her heart as she remembered her dream.

"Halt! You are entering United States government property. State your business." The soldier held his rifle across his chest as if ready to use it should it be necessary.

Sarah glanced through sore eyes at Tsula waiting for his approval to speak. She was not sure who to trust at this moment, but for now Tsula was the one protecting her from both soldier and tribesmen. Any one of them was capable of starting a bloodbath, the likes she'd already been privy to.

"We come to speak with the one they call, Charles Reynolds." Tsula's voice boomed loud in the morning stillness.

"What business do you have with Mr. Reynolds?" The soldier volleyed back, shifting the rifle over his shoulder.

"We have his daughter; she wishes to speak with him." He turned acknowledging Sarah's presence.

"Ma'am? Is this true? Are you in fact, Mr. Reynolds daughter?" The soldier leaned to the side, peering around Tsula for a better glimpse. The gesture caused his rifle to slip and immediately the tribesmen poised, directing their arrows at the lone man.

Sarah held her breath as the soldier held Tsula's gaze.

"Tell them to stop and I will speak." She hurriedly tapped her palm to Tsula's back hoping to stave off another loss of life.

Though his stance was military, the soldiers face was

frozen with fear. Sarah wondered if he was very much older than she.

Tsula raised his hand and the arrows again lowered to his command. "You will bring Charles Reynolds outside."

The soldier's Adams apple bobbed as he swallowed and with slow deliberate steps he backed his way to the fort's front gate.

Sarah scanned the perimeter of the fort, knowing that already the soldiers were scrambling up the ladders to hide behind the solid wood-hewn wall.

Time stood still as they awaited the arrival of her father. She could sense the tension thick as the morning fog and she hoped that Tsula could keep control, this time, of his people.

"Let my daughter come forward," Charles Reynolds bellowed as he approached the cluster of Cherokee. His gait was full stride, unafraid and this side of belligerent— just as she remembered him.

Sarah shifted, readying to dismount when Tsula raised his hand. She froze, praying he would keep his word to talk over his disagreements. She glanced at the tower, seeing the line of soldiers who stood ready for the signal to fire. With a fierce determination that no blood would be spilled, she slid from the horse and stood next to Tsula's horse.

"There can be no more bloodshed, Father. I assured them you were a reasonable man. I promised that you would listen and hear what they have to say." She held her father's gaze seeing his fatherly concern give way to seething anger.

"Have they hurt you, Sarah?" he called to her, "in *any* way?"

He had not heard her. It was though what she'd said dissipated in the mist. She had no choice but to comply with his question. "They have been considerate of my well-being, Father." She glanced up at Tsula, whose gaze was fixed on the soldiers at the fort.

Her father waved to her. "Come inside. You need to rest from your traumatic experience. We will have the military physician take a look at you."

He turned as though the eight Cherokee did not exist.

Sarah stared at his back as he walked away. There had been no true display of happiness in seeing her, no joy that she was well and in one piece standing before him.

"Father." She stepped forward, but not far from Tsula's side. Somehow she felt safer, understanding his honor, and his only wish to save his people from these deadly attacks. She was not as certain of her father's honor. In truth, she was not sure she'd ever really known her father, except through the picture he painted in his smattering of letters.

But foremost in her heart, she didn't wish to see bloodshed on either side.

He turned with a raised brow, as if surprised she should still be lagging behind. The gesture sparked a memory of her childhood when she'd peek into his study to ask a question. She had more than enough now and intended to have some answers. "Father, is it true that the Cherokee along the river have been terrorized by white settlers?" Sarah held her father's steady gaze, seeing when it softened to certain smugness.

Charles Reynolds lifted his eyes to Tsula. "Is this what they filled your head with? Turning you against your own flesh and blood?" Color flushed in his neck as he sternly bit off his words.

Her hopes of reaching a compromise began a slow and sickening spiral downward.

"Sarah, my dear girl. You don't understand. These sav—people are responsible for the deaths of many."

In this she knew he spoke the truth, but what or who had aggravated the Cherokee to such dire resolutions? If there was nothing else she'd learned in the past days, it was the wilderness had its own brand of justice and that it came in many forms—some self-appointed.

"Then stop the night raids on their people." Though he'd yet to admit he had anything to do with them, Sarah knew deep in her heart he did. "It is *their* land we take as our own."

She took another step toward him and Tsula grabbed her arm.

"Let her go you savage, or I will not be held responsible for what may happen." Reynolds pinned Tsula with a ferocious look.

The soldiers leveled their rifles at the Cherokee contingency.

"Just as you have taken no responsibility for the suffering of our people or theft of our land." Tsula yanked Sarah back to his side.

The two men eyed each other in disdain.

"How many more will have to die before the white man is satisfied? Before the Cherokee are satisfied?" The voice came from behind Tsula and his men.

Sarah's attention whirled toward the familiar voice. White Eagle, astride his beautiful appaloosa approached at a reverent pace through the mist, across his lap lay Running Doe's body, the red stain of her blood saturating her brown and yellow calico dress.

"Our people have been slain because we refuse to leave our land. Now the Cherokee are divided with this new treaty." He held up his palm covered with his sister's blood, then turned it smearing it down his chest. "How many more, Tsula?"

White Eagle stopped next to Sarah, but his gaze stayed on Tsula. "The arrow pulled from her body is that of our people, once used only for hunting. It has taken the life of your betrothed, and of my sister."

Tsula dropped his hold of Sarah's arm and she bolted to White Eagle's side. "Can we help her? Perhaps the doctor insi—" She glanced at him and her heart twisted in frustration already knowing it was too late.

"Your people signed that Treaty. It was approved by the United States government," Reynolds interjected. "What more proof do you need that it is time for the government to come in and teach your people about being civil with one another?"

"It does not speak for all Cherokee, Charles Reynolds." Tsula's voice was without emotion as he turned to White Eagle. "I am sorry for the loss of Running Doe. She had no part in this."

"Nor did the men and women you and your men killed that day," White Eagle responded.

The views of three human beings stood at the crossroads of destiny. Her gaze darted from her father to Tsula. "I want no part of either nation, if this is how it is to be governed."

White Eagle glanced at Tsula, and then to Charles Reynolds before he looked down at Sarah. "You are free to do as your spirit tells you. I will not stop you." He shifted his sister in his arms, his expression one of great sadness.

"Where will you go?" she whispered, brushing away a wisp of hair from Running Doe's gentle face. Sorrow clogged her throat.

His eyes so changeable with his moods, gazed on her with warmth. "I will go to my people. This is my vision. I must find a way to keep the old ways of the Cherokee strong and we must find a way to work together with the white man." He glanced at her father.

She could see the truth in what he said, but she had a feeling it would take much time—if ever—to truly achieve.

"Sarah, we must go inside now. Come."

She looked back at her father who now stood only a respectable pace from Tsula and his men. In her heart, she knew that neither Tsula, her father—or those like them—would be satisfied until they'd achieved their singular goals.

Reynolds frowned at Tsula. "I will do what I can to make sure that you and your men will receive a fair trial for this recent incident."

"As we will see you tried with fairness in a council of the clans, Charles Reynolds." Tsula glared at Sarah's father as he raised his hand to his men. "We will meet again, Charles Reynolds." He gently nudged his horse close to White Eagle and reached for Running Doe. "I beg for the honor of giving her a farewell ceremony. It is my duty and it is my privilege."

White Eagle hesitated then lifted his sister into the great man's arms.

He ran his fingers over her face, now pale and cold. "My heart mourns our loss, but it cannot change my vision." He captured White Eagle's gaze. "It will serve only to make it stronger."

"There are other ways," White Eagle urged.

"I will leave that to you, White Eagle. Do you wish us to stay?"

White Eagle shook his head solemnly.

He twisted towards his men and ushered them to follow.

Immediately, soldiers popped up over the wall and Sarah heard the repeated clicks of rifles being set to fire.

She edged near to White Eagle, laying her hand on his leg as they watched Tsula and his men disappear in the shrouded mist.

"Now, Sarah. Let us go inside." The terse tone in her father's voice confirmed her belief. He would always hold hostility for the Cherokee people.

Reynolds raised his hand, waving the soldiers to lower their rifles.

"Your place is with your people, Sarah Reynolds," White Eagle issued with a gentle command.

Sarah grasped his hand, tacky with the blood of his sister. "It is possible that I carry your child." She could not bring herself to look upon his face; afraid she would see only a compassionate dismissal.

Two fingers lifted her tear-stained face. "Running Doe said I would understand what it was to be a father." He shook his head. "I cannot risk losing you, Sarah. Better to know you are safe in your world, then what awaits my people."

She pressed his hand to her cheek. Tears rolled down her cheeks. "*You* are my world—my people. I will teach our children about the white man's world and you will instruct him in the Cherokee ways."

His smile, still sad, held a flicker of hope. He narrowed his gaze searching her eyes. "Sarah, understand what you are saying. Our people may not return to this land for many years."

"Sarah, I demand you come with me now. This is not why I wanted the finest education in the land for you. It is not why I paid good money to have you brought here to teach in the schools we will build." Her father's face turned purple with rage.

"To teach, father? Isn't that what you planned? I am still learning and what I see is a closed mind. One who has stopped learning."

Sarah straightened her shoulders. "May I trouble you for a horse, father?"

Charles Reynolds stared at his daughter as though she was out of her mind. "You don't really wish to do this, Sarah. You are overcome with emotion. Come now, be reasonable."

She knew then in her heart that she was never really a part of his life. He'd planned for her education in hopes it would help to further his cause and make his presence more known and respected among the white settlers of like minds.

In truth, all she'd learned about people, she'd gained from those closest to her. The loyal companionship from Emily gave her respect for herself, and the encouragement of her talents from Miss Emma. Compassion she'd learned from Running Doe and love she'd learned from White Eagle.

"Be wise in this, Sarah. I cannot promise you a white man's home."

She gazed up at him, ready to follow him if he would take her as she was. "Can you promise to teach our children honor and respect for all men?"

His dark eyes sparkled with challenge. He knew she'd made her choice.

He nodded. "Yes, I will promise you that and I will promise to love you to the end of our days."

"This is absurd, I forbid this. If you do this, Sarah, it will be the very last thing you ask of me." Her father planted his fists to his hips, taking on an authoritative stance that probably served to intimidate others.

Not his daughter. "A horse, please, father."

CHAPTER NINETEEN

New Beginnings

The fire burned bright within the sacred ceremonial ring. For seven long days the women had blessed the constant flame, preparing for the marriage to take place.

He'd faced many challenges in his lifetime, but White Eagle was certain that this waiting surpassed them all.

Two weeks since Sarah had given up all she'd known as her previous life, they'd gone quickly to the task of performing the ceremonial burial of Running Doe, placing her on a hillside overlooking the valley she once played in as a child.

In the spring, the tall grass swayed in the breeze through the profusion of white daisies and in the autumn, the grass turned to a brilliant cloak of gold against the blue sky. At the crest of the hill, a great oak tree stood, its branches gnarled, yet it still held a few leaves from year to year. Running Doe had often insisted that her brother help her up to the higher branches so she could survey the beauty of Mother Earth.

White Eagle stood next to Sarah that day as they stared down at the fresh mound of dirt that served as Running Doe's resting place. "She came here to gather flowers for weaving." He gave a broken chuckle. "My mother forced me to wear the rings she made, saying I should never turn away a gift of the heart."

Tsula, who had wanted to take part in the burial nodded, then quietly spoke, his voice tinged with emotion. "I remember, she possessed a special spirit, your sister."

Sarah placed a handful of daisies on the simple grave, her lips moving in silent prayer. She touched White Eagle's arm, almost healed now. In a few months' time, he would regain full strength from his wound.

"We shall bring our children here and tell them the stories of Running Doe." She pushed her dark hair from her face and smiled at White Eagle.

Despite his sorrow, the thought made White Eagle smile, then his mouth formed a thin line as he held back his tears. "She would have loved to teach you our ways." He captured Sarah's gaze, her face breathtakingly radiant with the small changes already happening to her body.

"I must leave you now, my brother." With a heavy sigh, Tsula walked to White Eagle and grasped his forearm in a gesture of friendship.

"Be well, my brother." White Eagle was grateful to have discovered that Running Doe's death had been avenged. Perhaps, in some ways, the Cherokee code had been honored. It was at least a measure of comfort in a small way to know that the perpetrator had not been one of Tsula's men.

"I go now to join Tsali and his men. I have heard of their efforts to help our people. Perhaps together we can do more good." He dropped his hand. "With the blessing of the Great Spirit, there is hope we shall find peace one day for our people."

White Eagle pulled Sarah closer into the crook of his arm. All the peace he needed was right here, with her. The legacy of his people had a future within her belly.

"May the Great Spirit guide you." With his bride-to-be

at his side, White Eagle's gaze followed Tsula as he rode away.

In his spirit, White Eagle sensed it would be the last time he would see his friend. He knew the killing would not stop on either side, not at least anytime soon. The Cherokee Nation was being divided, making it difficult for many to survive as they once had. No matter what sanctions the United States government ordered, there would be those who would benefit and those who would not. As long as the code of the Cherokee stood as the only accepted form of justice, the white man would not approve of it.

His heart grieved for what he'd seen in his dreams and that his people would continue to suffer greater sorrows in the days to come. He'd seen the long lines of his people trailing over the valleys and plains, trudging through the wintry mix of ice and snow. He'd seen the children left behind, crying for their mothers. He'd seen the numbers of those who died unable to make the perilous journey.

His visions had revealed too, his role. Someone would need to gather the orphaned children; someone would need to hold the bits and pieces of the remaining clans together until the great storm passed.

Through the small, scattered remains of the various clans and through the children of his seed, honor and peace would one day come again to the Cherokee nation.

"You are far from here, my love." Sarah gazed up at him, her hair blowing free in the late autumn breeze.

"Have I told you today how very brave you are?" He brushed the hair from her face, cradling her cheek in his hand. "How my heart lifts when you smile?"

She leaned against his hand and his heart filled with

joy. "If I have learned bravery, it is you who has been my teacher and it is my hope that my smile will serve always to lift your heart."

He grew serious as he studied her face. Did she realize when she gave up her home, that all she'd thought secure in her life would become so uncertain? "There is much ahead that we will need to be brave for, my Sarah."

"It will be well." She touched his cheek, placing a gentle kiss to his lips, and then turned her attention to scan the view from the hillside. "It will be well, my love, you will see."

∞

The crisp autumn twilight offered its gift of purple, yellow, and orange streaks across the evening sky. Nature's palette for the backdrop of a day White Eagle had only been able to envision in his dreams.

With many thoughts running through his mind, he walked towards the ceremonial fire with a blue blanket wrapped loosely around his shoulders. In the stars beginning to dot the twilight sky, the spirit of Running Doe was clearly present. Ideally, this would have been the time she and Tsula would have taken their vows before the tribal clans.

From the other side of the small group encircling the fire, Sarah emerged, wrapped also in a blanket of blue. Her dark hair cascaded in soft curls over her shoulders, her warm gaze with those emerald eyes, sparkled with a love and anticipation.

The Shaman uttered, in the Native tongue, his words of blessing, raising his hands to call upon the spirits and those gathered to raise their voices in song.

White Eagle's memory thrust back to a few weeks before when they'd stood before one another. Aware of the precious gift the gods had bestowed on him, he took pleasure of the total look of trust in her eyes.

The fire snapped, dancing in celebration as the sky darkened and the stars illuminated the sky.

He held Sarah's gaze, the words of the Shaman hopelessly lost as he memorized every nuance of her beautiful face. White Eagle swallowed to remind himself this was not a dream. This was his Sarah, in the flesh, soon to be his wife.

Aware suddenly of a tugging at his elbow, he realized the Shaman was trying to remove the blanket. Caught in his daydream, White Eagle glanced sheepishly at the old man and noted the Shaman's raised brow as he relinquished the blue blanket.

"Now the ceremonial blanket." He raised his hands and two women scurried forward, presenting the snow-white blanket to the elderly man.

Their slight tittering of nervous laughter followed as they departed in as much haste as they'd arrived.

The touch of Sarah's fingers sliding into his palm startled White Eagle. He looked down and found her dressed in a simple doeskin shift and his heart stilled at her beauty.

The Shaman offered him a knowing smile as he wrapped the blanket around them, signifying the union was nearly complete in the eyes of the Great Spirit.

He held tight their clasped hands and raised his face to the sky chanting for the spirits to grant them a full and prosperous life together. He then raised his hands to the heavens and proclaimed in loud declaration a blessing on the newly wedded couple.

When he was finished, he nodded toward White Eagle. "You may speak."

White Eagle swallowed. "Our new life together has started, my Sarah. I will cherish you to the end of my days."

The Shaman nodded toward Sarah.

"My heart is and always will be yours."

White Eagle bent down touching his lips gently to that of his new bride.

Later, they stole away from the joyous nightlong celebration, finding privacy in the special ceremonial hut that had been built for their wedding night.

"Please do not tell me that already you are having second thoughts about your new wife?" Sarah emerged, wrapped only in the white ceremonial blanket from the entrance to the hut that had been built for their wedding night.

Against the bright full moon, her new husband stood staring up at the night sky.

He glanced over his shoulder with a smile, and accepting her into his arms, drew her close. She wrapped her arms around his waist and again, her soul found peace and contentment in being near him. She pressed her cheek against his bare shoulder, cherishing the recent hours they'd spent celebrating their marriage.

"My father told me once that the numbers of the stars represent all the people of the Cherokee clans." His body was warm, strong against hers. "As a boy, on my journey to manhood, I found comfort whenever I looked to the heavens."

For a moment they stared at the expanse of ebony sky littered with diamond-like stars.

"Would he be pleased with me, White Eagle?"

"My father?" He smiled at her, shedding all her concern with a single look. "He would be proud of you, my Sarah." A gentle sigh escaped his lips as he pulled her close, resting his chin on the top of her head. "He would be proud and honored to have you as my wife."

"And your mother, would she have approved?"

"She was a brave woman, like you. Yes, she would have been proud to have you in our family."

With her cheek resting against the chiseled warmth of his chest, she smiled believing her mother would have also been pleased with her choices. "I think I would have liked your mother." She glanced up catching the fine plane of his firm jaw. "Just look how well you turned out."

He chuckled, squeezing her briefly before leaning back to catch her gaze. "They approve, my entire family. Look to the heavens." He held her with one arm as he waved the other across the star-studded sky. "Does not the sky sparkle with joy this night?"

"It does and my heart is filled with such happiness."

"And you do not miss your family?" He pulled her close, wrapping her tight in his arms. Sarah knew *this* was home.

"You are my family, you, Isabella, and…" she glanced at her still flat belly, touching it gingerly. Her suspicions confirmed by the Shaman, she was pregnant with White Eagles child. She returned her gaze to his and smiled.

"You are no longer the shy girl in the cave."

"But you are the same man who stole glances my way when you thought I wasn't looking."

"You made it difficult to ignore you."

"I did no such thing. Can I help you were smitten from

the moment you awoke from your delirium?"

"Perhaps I was enchanted under a spell." He ran his finger along the edge of the blanket, easing open the folds until she stood before him, her arms outstretched. His gaze took a slow and appreciative appraisal of what lay beneath the blanket. "Knowing you carry our child makes you even more enchanting."

He scooped her into his arms, turning toward the hut. "What is this odd gesture your friend, Emily taught you about earlobes?"

Sarah obliged him by nibbling along the edge, and moving down the corded strength of his neck. She was pleased to feel his body tighten in response.

"That?"

"Remind me to thank her one day."

"I don't think so, *Mr.* White Eagle." She pulled back turning his face to hers as they walked over the threshold. "I've experienced your method of thanks."

His brow rose and a half-grin played on his face. "Then I will personally thank you for being so willing to learn."

"I am a teacher, after all, and always willing to learn."

He laid her on the tufted pallet, his gaze running hot over her as she opened the blanket.

"Then I will teach you what I know." He traced his finger slowly between her breasts as her body caught fire as always under his touch.

Sarah sighed, closing her eyes to the quickening of sensations. "And who shall I have to thank for this knowledge?" Her breath caught as his mouth found hers.

"We will thank each other," he whispered against her mouth before capturing it and her heart again.

EPILOGUE

Six years later

Sarah ruffled the thick tufts of ebony hair on her son's head, as he smiled at her. His dark eyes glittered like water splashing over river rock—just like his father's. The child, already seven months in her belly, stirred as if he knew his brother was nearby.

"Mama?" Isabella expertly wove one daisy stem after another as she spoke, "tell me again the rose story."

Though Sarah's skin had grown accustomed to the bright heat of the sun, it was still not thick enough, nor would it ever be, to recount the legend of the Cherokee rose.

She brushed her hair over her shoulders, creating a quick single braid that hung low on her back. "I will tell it once more, but only if you will braid some flowers for my hair." The baby turned again causing her to pause, catching her breath.

"Your little brother is active today." She smiled and held her hand out to the closest thing to a daughter she had.

Isabella's bright blue eyes sparkled with glee. "How can the old women tell that it's a boy, mama?" She scrambled to her feet, grasping her mother's hand, and then plopped down on the blanket, behind her mother.

"The old women are very wise, Izzy. They have been delivering babies for many generations."

Sarah scanned the vast hillside, blanketed with daisies. Nearby, the simple white cross of Running Doe's grave held a freshly woven wreath of wildflowers.

Most times, it was as though Sarah had lived here forever, the traditions were so engrained in her spirit.

A warm wind blew across her face as her attention was pulled back to the story her daughter had asked her to tell. A story of courage and heartache, told to her by the elders who'd escaped to the mountains shortly after her marriage to White Eagle.

"In late summer, the story says the mothers of the Cherokee children who had to leave their homes, cried so much in their grief because they were unable to help their children survive the long and perilous journey in the winter months. The elders prayed for a sign that would lift the mother's spirits to give them strength."

Sarah paused as Little Eagle shifted, laying his head in his mother's lap. Smiling at his sweet profile, she covered the edge of his face with her hand, blocking out the harsh rays of the sun.

"Go on, Mama. Tell the part about the tears turning into flowers."

Her heart ached whenever she told the story. White Eagle had only been able to convince a few to escape from the horrific visions he'd foreseen in his dreams. So many more died during the forced emigration, many were not allowed to take anything other than what they were able to snatch as they were prodded by soldiers with guns to evacuate their homes.

Sarah's eyes welled with the memory. "The story says the elders prayed and the next day as they walked, a beautiful rose began to grow where each mother's tear fell to the ground. Legend says that a trail of roses now grows along the entire emigration route."

"Tell me again what the roses look like, Mama, so I don't forget."

Sarah's heart twisted at her daughter's innocence, yet with the legend she hoped Isabella, Little Eagle, and others would never forget. "They say they are white, which represents the purity of tears, and that they have a gold center, to depict the gold taken from the Cherokee land. Legend says they have seven leaves on each stem that represents the seven original Cherokee clans."

"I'm trying to teach the clan names to Little Eagle, but he isn't using his English very well." She leaned over Sarah's shoulder and stared at her brother.

"Be patient with him, Izzy. He is young."

"We will ever get to see the trail, mama?" Isabella's gentle hands tugged at Sarah's hair, brushing soft against the back of her neck.

"Perhaps one day, when things are more settled." She wondered when, and if, that day would truly ever come.

"That story is so sad, mama. Have you ever cried?"

Sarah smiled, but with a melancholy heart. In her barely twenty-five years on this earth, Sarah had seen more than her share of tears.

Her mind flipped through the pages of her memory, like a book recalling the times when she'd had to make the choice to be brave. The night White Eagle had taken her to view the stars high in the hills away from the village and told her that news had come of her father's death. Sarah had wept for the father she'd never truly known and said a prayer of silent thanks that her children would know their father.

Odd that fate had led her and White Eagle in full circle to find each other.

In a bout of irony, it was not until sometime after, that she received word of the large inheritance left to her by her father. With little discussion, she and White Eagle gave the money to Chief Ross and the Nation for his proposed idea of building schools to educate those Cherokee children orphaned by the forced emigration.

Still, more disturbing news was to follow. They would hear of Tsula's death, along with another warrior, and Tsali the man well known among his people for striving for justice among the white settlers and the military. They had given up their lives in the tradition of the Cherokee after allegedly killing a guard whom they'd observed beating a young Indian woman.

There were times during those dismal days when Sarah feared her crying would ever cease.

She reached for the child who had not yet questioned why her hair color was not dark—but blonde and curly, nor wondered why her eyes were blue as the sky while her brothers were dark as night.

"I have wept many times, but it is the sound of laughter I would rather hear." She tickled the young girl's sides, laughing as she collapsed in a fit of giggles, sparking the avid interest of her brother to join in.

Rolling in the grass is where White Eagle found them. "I can see you are teaching my children about serious matters."

Sarah raised her hand over her brow shading her eyes to see his expression.

His grin met hers.

"I will leave the serious subjects for us to discuss later,

my husband."

One lone eyebrow arched on his handsome face.

"For now, come sit with us and tell the story of Running Doe's encounter with the snake and what she chose to do with it." Sarah smiled pleasantly.

White Eagle leaned over his son and kissed her softly, then glanced down placing a gentle hand on her belly.

She pulled the worn journal, its pages folded haphazard between its bindings from beneath her skirts.

"You've not recorded this one?" Her husband sat next to her, his hand still resting on her belly.

"I heard from Emily two weeks ago. She asked for more stories. She says she is working hard to convince the Tribune to publish them." She shrugged. "You never know, perhaps one day the Cherokee Nation will have their own newspaper. Wasn't it a wise Cherokee that once said, 'you cannot stop fate?'"

"Fate, it would appear my lovely wife, bears the most beautiful green eyes, carries a wit sharp as an adder, and—"

"Your children." She tapped his nose with her pencil.

"Isabella, take your brother down to the village. I smelled fresh fry cake as I came up the hill. See if the women will let you and your brother sample one in the cool shade."

Isabella grabbed her little brother's hand and bounded with him down the hill, their laughter trailing behind them.

"Be polite!" he called after them and Isabella paused long enough to give her father a wide smile of assurance.

"Thank you for reminding them." Sarah struggled to her knees, giving a great sigh in her attempt to stand.

"Your son is growing rapidly."

White Eagle stood, lifting her under the arms until she could balance her stance on her own.

Sarah covered her eyes from the glare of the sun, as they watched their children being greeted by the open arms of the old women in the tribe.

"Now, what was it that you wished to discuss with me that required sending our children away?"

"Perhaps I simply wished to be alone with my wife." White Eagle wrapped his arms around her from behind, unable to make his fingertips meet over her belly. "Are you sure there is only one child that you carry?"

She slapped his forearm. "This is your heritage you speak of, Mr. White Eagle."

He turned her to face him, tipping her chin to meet his loving gaze. "No, Mrs. White Eagle, this is *our* heritage."

NOTES FROM THE AUTHOR:

I had always thought that one day I might release this book again (published in 2005 as White Eagles Lady) Its timeless message rings true even today, showing that no matter what the circumstances, love will always find a way. I hope you've enjoyed A Warriors Heart and I invite you to learn more about the Cherokee history and the great things happening today in the Cherokee nation~ Amanda

∞

Many wonderful resources depict the historical beginnings and evolution of the Cherokee nation. Some of those I found especially helpful are:

The Cherokees
By Grace Woodward
ISBN# 0-8061-1815-6
University of Oklahoma Press, Norman Publishing Division

The Official site of the Cherokee Nation
(Tahlequah, Oklahoma)

http://www.Cherokee.org/

This website is an exquisitely well-kept site depicting many historical, educational, cultural, and informative links. I owe much of my background research to this site and its newsletter, the Cherokee Nation Newsletter. I encourage you to find out yourself what a wealth of information there is to this site.

CHEROKEE CLAN SYSTEM:

Historically, the Cherokee society is a matrilineal society. For many generations, women were considered the head of their household, with her home and children left to her in the event of separation from her husband. There are many valid reasons for understanding the continued traditional divisions of the original seven clans. You can research each clan and its subdivisions at **http://www. cherokee.org** .

The original seven clans consist of the following:
A-ni-gi-lo-hi (Longhair)
A-ni-a-wi (Deer)
A-ni-go-te-ga-wi (Wild Potato)
A-ni-sa-ho-ni (Blue)
A-ni-wa-ya (Wolf)
A-ni-tsi_squa (Bird)
A-ni-wo-di (Paint)

GLOSSARY OF CHEROKEE TERMS:

E du j (uncle)
E lohi (earth)
Svn oyi (night)
Nvdo iga ehi (sun)
Dit lohisdi (encounter)
Soquili (horse)
Adanvdo (heart/spirit)
Ugeyudi (lovely)
Gvgeyui (love)
Uweyv (river)
Svnoyi echi nvdo (moon)
Wa-do (thank you)
Uwolvtsadi (clever)
Tsula (fox)
Duyukta the straight and narrow path

HERBS COMMON TO THE CHEROKEE COUNTRY:

http://www.cherokee.org

The owners of this website note that uses for these and other herbs may vary from clan to clan, as well as through periods of history. **Uses listed here are for the purpose of historical fiction only and offer no credence in any way to their effectiveness. Do not attempt such procedures on your own accord-as in any serious medical emergency.

Squirrel Tail, Saloli gatogo (Yarrow)

Once used for many uses, one of its best known was to stop excess bleeding by way of a poultice or pack to the wound.

Qua lo ga Sumac) Staghorn Sumac

All parts of the common sumac have medicinal use. Sometimes used as a gargle for sore throats, or as a remedy for diarrhea. The tea made from its crushed leaves and berries was sometimes used to reduce fevers.

Echinacea-The purple Coneflower

Crushed coneflower made as a poultice was sometimes used as a means to draw poison from snakebite or other poisonous wounds.

ABOUT THE AUTHOR

Amanda McIntyre's storytelling is a natural offshoot of her artistic creativity.

A visual writer, living in the rich tapestry of the American heartland, her passion is telling character-driven stories with a penchant (okay, some call it a wicked obsession) for placing ordinary people in extraordinary situations to see how they overcome the obstacles to their HEA.

A bestselling author, her work is published internationally in Print, E-book, and Audio. She writes steamy contemporary and sizzling historical romance and truly believes, no matter what, love will always find a way.

Learn more and get connected at:
www.amandamcintyresbooks.com

AMAZON.USA AUTHOR:
www.amazon.com/author/amandamcintyre

AMAZON .uk AUTHOR PAGE:
www.amazon.co.uk/-/e/B002C1KH2Q

NEWSLETTER:
http://madmimi.com/signups/110714/join

OTHER BOOKS BY AMANDA MCINTYRE:

CONTEMPORARY ROMANCE:
Wild at Heart (Wild Irish Kindle World. April 2017)
Thunderstruck (Hell Yeah Kindle World Nov. 2016))
Going Home (Sapphire Falls Kindle World Oct 2016)
All I Want for Christmas (holiday novella)
No Strings Attached, Book I (Last Hope Ranch)
Rugged Hearts, Book I (Kinnison Legacy)
Rustler's Heart, Book II (Kinnison Legacy
Renegade Hearts, Book III (Kinnison Legacy)
Stranger in Paradise
Tides of Autumn
Unfinished Dreams
Wish You Were Here
Historical Erotic Thriller:
The Dark Seduction of Miss Jane
Historical/Erotic Romance:
The Master & the Muses *
The Diary of Cozette *
Tortured *
The Pleasure Garden *
Winter's Desire *
Dark Pleasures *
*Starred titles available in audio and international languages

CONTEMPORARY ADULT FICTION:
Private Party
Mirror, Mirror

Naughty Bits, Vol III
Historical time-travel:
Closer To You (formerly Wild & Unruly)
Christmas Angel (formerly Fallen Angel)
Para/Fantasy:
Tirnan 'Oge